THE FAITH OF
A Collie

ALBERT PAYSON TERHUNE

THE FAITH OF
A Collie

Grosset & Dunlap
PUBLISHERS
NEW YORK

Printed in the United States of America
By arrangement with Harper & Brothers

MY BOOK
IS DEDICATED TO MY OLD FRIEND
Robert T. Sheldon
(of "Fox Hall")

THE FAITH OF
A Collie

CHAPTER

1

NOW a letter makes dull enough reading to outsiders. Most of all when its writer has been dead for some hundred-and-twenty-odd years.

Yet in a few minutes I must ask you to read such a letter; and to read it through, without skipping. For on it depend many of the strange happenings you will find in this story of mine.

Up in the lake country of northern New Jersey are two tumbles of mountain range—one stretching to the Hudson, the other rolling brokenly westward.

They are spurs of the Blue Ridge. The two ranges are split by a rich farmland valley, through which wanders the Ramapo River that empties at last into Pompton Lake.

In this Ramapo Valley, at the very edge of the narrow river and all but in the shadow of the westward tumble of mountains, lies the old Hardin farm, with its pre-Revolutionary house and its pleasant meadows and woodland. For six generations, the Hardins have lived there.

In this house Bruce Hardin was born. From it he went to New York, where he was winning a fair way for himself in business, when in 1917 he crossed the gray Atlantic with some two million other young Americans, to do his part in the first World War.

Two years later he came back, weak from three wounds and suffering mildly from shell-shock.

To build up his cracked health, he turned from the city to his home at the old Hardin farm, in the Ramapos.

He had no intention of staying long in the mountain country, but the love of the soil crept back upon him. In time he was once more the rugged athlete of other days. But he stayed on at the family homestead, going in seriously for scientific farming.

With him lived his chum and war-comrade, Horace Bladen, a geologist of note, who, like Bruce, had been smashed in health by the war and who welcomed the peaceful haven of Hardin Farm, for the convalescent months that followed.

Bruce and Bladen lived right pleasantly there, on the river-edge and in the shadow of the high-piled mountains. They were congenial. They were young. They were busy. They were taken into ready friendship by the other farmers, up and down the valley.

Their next-door neighbor, a quarter-mile away, was Ethan Wallace, a well-to-do dairyman. At the Wallace home boarded Sibyl Gates, a twenty-four-year-old school-teacher, who had been sent by a benevolent society to do uplift work and to teach, amid the scattered mountain settlements to west of the river.

It was no easy task for the girl. It had been still less easy for other teachers and settlement workers who had preceded her. For these Ramapo mountaineers, to a great extent, were as primitive as savages. Born and bred within thirty miles of New York City, many of them could not read or write, and many had an outlook on life at large that would have shamed a half-wit.

"Jackson Whites" they were called in the valley, where tales of their ignorance and lawlessness were rife.

A mile or so farther back in the mountains dwelt a group of mountaineers whom the Jackson Whites looked down on as contemptuously as the valley farmers looked down on the Jackson Whites.

These were the "Blue-eyed Niggers," a queer blend of mixed races which had kept their type intact for more than a century by intermarriage and by isolation.

In aspect these Blue-eyed Niggers resembled East Indians more than any other race; except that their eyes were a light and brilliant blue. Slender, swarthy, furtive, coppery of complexion, they lived their own hidden lives among the mountain fastnesses, seldom venturing forth to Oakland or Pompton or Mahwah or other of the valley towns.

They were an ancient blend of Negro and Indian and German. How these three races chanced to mix will be told in the letter of which I have spoken.

Your story begins in the early spring of 1923.

Bruce Hardin had been taking advantage of a rainy

morning to overhaul a mass of junk in the homestead garret. Downstairs, Bladen was hard at work on a paper for the *Geological Monthly*.

Bladen was interrupted in his writing by a visit from Ethan Wallace, his next-door neighbor, who had come across to see Bruce about the joint hiring of a tractor from a farmer up the valley.

With Wallace was Sibyl Gates. She had brought back a book she had borrowed from Bladen.

Hearing Sibyl's voice in the living-room below, Bruce started up eagerly from the perusal of a handful of old and yellowed papers he had exhumed from a haircloth trunk. The sound of her voice had begun to have an unaccountable effect on him lately, though he himself did not wholly realize it.

Downstairs he ran, brushing the dust from his hands and clothes as he went, and carrying one of the several letters he had been poring over.

"Why, hello!" he greeted Sibyl. "How does it happen you are taking a holiday to-day? I supposed you were up yonder, trying to persuade the Jackson White children that the alphabet is not a magic spell, and teaching their loving mothers that babies won't necessarily catch cold if their faces are washed."

"This is Saturday," Sibyl reminded him. "The one basic truth of education that I've been able to make them grasp, thus far, is that Saturday is a holiday. They never forget that, even if they do forget that 'cat' is not spelled with a 'k.' I've brought back Mr. Bladen's *History of Bergen County*. I borrowed it in the hope I could find something that would appeal to the children's local spirit. But I——"

[4]

"I've something here that will appeal more to it," interposed Bruce. "Or at least it would, if they had any. It's a human document about their own home region, not merely their own county. By the way, Wallace, this will interest you, too, after all the study you've been making of neighborhood history."

"Another book of——?"

"It's a letter I ran across in the attic this morning, along with a sheaf of others, in a haircloth trunk that must be a million years old. The paper is pretty yellow and brittle and the ink is pale. But I managed to make it out. Like to hear it? It's rather interesting."

Encouraged by the triple assent, Bruce unfolded gingerly the fragile pages and went to the window, where the light was stronger.

"This is dated July 11, 1780," prefaced Bruce. "It was written by my great-grandfather, old Colonel Standish Hardin, to his wife. He was with Washington's army, you know, and she was here, at home. There are more than a dozen of his letters to her in the same trunk. Letters were a rarity in those days and she seems to have saved all his. I don't know why. For there is hardly a word of intimacy or affection in any of them, and every one begins: 'Honored Madam.' But——"

"That was how men wrote to their womenfolks back in the Revolution," put in Wallace. "I've got a swad of letters from my great-grandfather to his wife. I remember one of 'em is dated from Morristown, when Washington had his headquarters there. It begins something like this:

" 'Honored Madam:—These soldier-folk be parlous drunken and profane ruffians, and they do horrify me with

[5]

their loose and godless ways. I pray you send me by express messenger a cask of our own good home-made rum, for this army grog be not fit to wash a dog in.' He——"

"This letter of my great-grandfather's is not written from Morristown," said Bruce, "though he had been stationed there, on Washington's staff. He was on special detail with General Anthony Wayne when he wrote this—'Mad Anthony,' you know. It's dated from Tarrytown. Most of his other letters are from Morristown, though. Shall I read it?"

Without waiting for reply this time, he turned to his handful of yellowed pages again.

A huge gold-red collie dog came into the room in leisurely fashion, having followed Bruce to the attic and waking from a snooze there to find him gone.

In search of his master, the dog entered, glancing in mild inquiry at the visitors, then crossing to where Sibyl Gates sat and thrusting his classic silken head under her welcomingly outstretched hand.

"Lie down, Mars," gently commanded the girl, petting the collie's head and accepting his gravely proffered white paw. "Your master is going to read aloud to you. I'm sure you'll understand him ever so much better than the Jackson White children understand *me*. Listen."

The collie lay down majestically at her feet, in easy reach of her caressing fingers.

Sibyl was the only person, apart from Bruce and Bladen, in whom Mars deigned to take the slightest interest and whom he made any pretense of obeying. Bruce had noted with unconscious delight this fondness of his exclusive collie for the young teacher.

[6]

As the dog stretched himself at Sibyl's feet, Hardin began to read:

"The Eleventh July, 1780. Given at Tarrytown, where I serve for the time with Gen. A. Wayne. To my wife.

"Honored Madam: Greetings and these:

"I had hoped to surprise you with a sudden visit to our dear home, this past sevennight; where reports of crops and of profits show that my overseer stands in some need of my presence and of a stout reproof for certain gross derelictions of business.

"Also I had hoped to see yourself and the children.

"But Providence hath ordered it otherwise; though I rode within two leagues of mine own house. And here I be at the Tarrytown headquarters with a Hessian bullet through the calf of my left leg; while better men do serve our country in the field.

"It befell in this wise:

"From my last express, you are aware that the British at New York have been preparing to march in force upon Morristown (in two detachments, so our spies inform us; one through Springfield and one by Milburn.)

"So confident are they of success against our smaller force that in New York, these spies report, it is believed that Morristown hath assuredly fallen to them ere now and that the next express will bring tidings of British occupation there."

"Like blazes it was!" cut in Wallace. "I read all about that march on Morristown. They called it a 'triumph march.' At Springfield and again on this side of Milburn, Washington's Jersey troops met the two bodies of redcoats, and sent both of 'em scuttling back to New York on the

run. They never had a chance to reach Morristown. They
———. Excuse me, Hardin," he interrupted himself. "Go
ahead with your reading."

Bruce resumed:

"So certain were the military authorities in New York
that Morristown had fallen, that, six day ago, they dispatched thither a pay chest, to the division paymaster,
along with divers military orders to the general in command.

"They sent it under escort of a battalion of Hessians.
These followed in the wake of the main army's march, but
farther to northward, to avoid chance bands of patriots.
Private dispatches were sent along by certain Tories and by
the relatives of officers on the main expedition.

"Among these was a casket, forwarded by the wife of
one Major Hough (of King George's 99th Foot Regiment)
to her husband at Morristown. For some cause, Hough had
sent back an express to his wife to collect all the money
and other valuables she might lay hands on and to send
them after him by trusty messenger, so soon as news should
come that Morristown was captured by the British and
that he was alive there.

"This wife, it appears, took for granted the town must
fall. So, not waiting, she sent forward the money, etc., along
with the pay-chest, under this strong escort of Hessians.

"Why Maj. Hough should want so vast a store of wealth
in money and jewels and the like, in so God-forsaken a
region, I cannot guess; unless he hath lost so much at
gaming, with his brother officers, that he must needs throw
all his riches into the deficit or else be disgraced. Or it may

be he seeks to take up a land grant, thereabouts from some Dutch patroon.

"But in any event, he so ordered; and she so obeyed, albeit with overmuch precipitancy as you shall see.

"Our spies bore word to General Wayne of the secret march of the Hessian battalion, with the treasure. On the minute, he crosseth the Hudson with three hundred of his 'Riders'—and he granteth me leave to join the foray.

"We fell upon the Hessian escort, just before daylight, a mile to the south of Pompton; where they were bivouacked in a great *vlei*."

"A *vlei* is the Jersey Dutch word for meadow," put in Wallace. " '*Bog en Vlei*' is the old name for that marsh-and-meadow tract below Pompton Plains. Go ahead."

"Madam," read on Bruce, "you know by common report the dashing attacks of 'Mad Anthony' Wayne's irregular horsemen. It was a privilege and a tactical education for me to ride with them on that foray.

"They scattered the Hessians like chaff. They rolled them up again and they smote them afresh, like the wrath of heaven. In a half-hour those of the German mercenaries who were not slain were captured.

"We lost barely nine men in all, in killed and wounded. But among the latter was I, with the aforetold flesh wound in my left leg's calf.

"Yet, despite our glorious victory, we had naught to show for our pains. For the pay chest and Maj. Hough's casket of jewels and money had vanished. Nor could they be found.

"Gen. Wayne had no time to squander. For there was

[9]

chance that a stronger body of British, from toward Morris-town, might be dispatched back to meet the Hessians.

"Therefore, after he had searched in vain for the plunder, he set his face toward Tarrytown again, with all speed, driving his captives before him and carrying his dead and wounded in farm carts he commandeered.

"Yet, this morning, word comes to me of a strange tale babbled by a Hessian trooper who hath broken down under much and vehement questioning.

"And this, Madam, after all the general's cross-questioning of the Hessian commander and his officers proved vain. It proved vain because they know naught. This trooper chanced to know all. This is the tale he tells:

"It seems he and three others were detailed to guard the chest and the casket, during the last watch of the night. When we swooped down on the Hessians before dawn, the command scattered in all directions, as I have related.

"These four men seized up their chest and casket and hid in the woods, lying close in a thicket, while the fight waged. As they hid there, one of them said:

" 'Why do we toil and moil and risk death and endure stripes and eat poor fare, while wealth lies in our grasp? Our comrades be in flight. Let us carry this treasure to the mountains; and there let us hide it. When King George hath won this war and hath crushed these colonist rebels—as he must within a handful of months at most—then can we come forth and we can smuggle our wealth back to Hesse-Cassel; and there we can live like great nobles for the rest of our days.'

"All agreed. To the north were the wilderness mountains

of the Ramapo, where there be, as we know, a thousand safe places to hide both man and gear.

"And thither they designed to go; so soon as the fighting should be over and their fellows slain or dispersed. Thither they planned to carry their booty and to hide it.

"In the meanwhile they lay safe hid in the thickets; and the flight and pursuit swept far beyond.

"One of the four—the leader—was named Groot. Another was one Devries; and a third was called Mann. The fourth—he who told the tale this morning—gives us his name as Schwartz.

"Now, in the stricken camp, Schwartz had left his knapsack, wherein was his lucky charm (though scant luck did it bring him, that day) and certain small moneys and trifles of loot that he had picked up in ransacked farmhouses and which he was loath to abandon.

"So while the others lay hid, he crept forth to find this knapsack, for the chase was yet a full mile off. He deemed it safe to slip out and get his knapsack and return again to his fellows and to the treasure they guarded.

"But while he was rummaging amid the litter of the stormed camp, a wounded man of Wayne's Riders lay there, having been shot from his horse when we charged the bivouac. This Rider lifted his carbine and fired upon Schwartz, who he thought was a camp-follower come back to pillage the patriot wounded.

"The ball grazed Schwartz's scalp, stunning him.

"There he lay, senseless, until we returned to search the camp. Then, coming to his senses, he sought to creep back to the thicket.

[11]

"But one of our men laid him by the heels and made him prisoner, thus putting to naught his dreams of treasure and of becoming a great noble in Hesse-Cassel—wherever that oddly-named far country may be.

"This then is the tale he hath told to our provost marshal, to-day. If it be a lie, he hath a truly fertile brain to devise it so ingeniously. If it be true, then, Madam, within a few miles of our home, at most, doth rest a goodly store of British gold; and a casket of money and of jewels as well.

"So soon as I can secure furlough, after my wound hath healed, I shall make post-haste for home and search right cannily for it.

"Knowing the Ramapos as I do, I misdoubt me not I shall find it. In the meantime, I conjure you, keep a still tongue, Madam, of all this.

"For I am not minded that every scatter-brain from Hackensack to the Pomptons should range the mountains in quest of it and, mayhap, with fool's luck, come upon it.

"And so, Honored Madam, I commend you and our children to the mercies of Providence; in the hope of an early reunion with you all.

"And I pray you berate my overseer roundly that he hath had so poor a report to send me of the winter wheat and of the new fruit trees.

"Nor, Madam, can I praise your own report of the household expenditures. It beseems me there hath been grievous waste there.

"I exhort you to read the 27th chapter of the Book of Proverbs, in Holy Writ, once more, and with care. I refer to the chapter wherein the Preacher doth describe a virtuous and careful house-wife who 'riseth while it is yet dark' and 'looketh well to the ways of her household and eateth not the bread of idleness' and who spendeth the day in wise supervision of her husband's home.

"I pray you to read and to profit. And so I sign myself

"Yr ob'dt servant and lov'g spouse,

"STANDISH HARDIN, Col. on His Exc'l'ncy's Staff; at present serving with Maj. Gen. A. Wayne."

Bruce laid down the yellowed letter with a laugh.

Ethan Wallace had scarce been able to remain silent through the final paragraphs. Fidgeting and sputtering, he burst forth, now:

"It's true, Hardin! It's all true! I heard about it when I was a kid. From granther. He had it from his mother. Not about the treasure—though there's always been rumors and yarns about money being hid up in those hills yonder. I've heard talk of it from the old folks; though I never took any stock in it.

"But the part that I know is true is about Groot and Devries and Mann. There were three Hessian deserters, with those names, that sneaked away from the British army, during the Revolution; and hid up in the Ramapo Mountains near here. It's even in one of the history books at Trenton. Everyone knows that. And everyone knows they lived in the Ramapos with some runaway black slaves—Jersey was a slave state in those times, you know— and with some renegade Lenape Indians. The three races intermarried. That's where the Blue-eyed Niggers come from."

"But——"

"The three Hessians lorded it over the coons and the redskins and made them wait on 'em hand and foot. That's history, too. They lived up there till they died. I figger they likely hid the pay-chest and the casket safe somewhere, before they got to fraternizing with the slaves and the Indians, and they never had a safe chance to realize on their wealth.

"America won the war, you see. The British left. The Hessians, too. So here were Groot and Devries and Mann, stranded high and dry, with no chance to cash in, or to smuggle their treasure back to Germany. The custom-house would have searched their luggage. It was too much of a risk. Men were hanged for theft in those days. And three backwoods Germans with a fortune in gold and jewelry would have been nabbed the minute they tried to get their wealth out of the country. The three knew it. They kept on laying low. It was the only thing they could do. That treasure is up there yet. It———"

"Hold on!" broke in Sibyl Gates, in eager excitement. "I can add a link to that! At least I can, if by some miracle Cleppy Bemis told me the truth. Cleppy comes nearer being normal than anyone else in the school. He has imagination, too, and brains, such as they are. But so many of his stories involve bears and ghosts that I've lost my simple faith in them. Still, this seems to fit in so well———"

"What does?" asked Bladen.

"Why," she answered, "one day he was walking home from school with me, along the ridge path, back of Bear Swamp. Down in a hollow, just below us, we saw a man on his hands and knees, fumbling among some crevices in the rocks, with a pick-ax. It was Tully Bemis—Cleppy's uncle, you know, that sour-faced mountaineer who comes past here sometimes with cordwood—the one with shoulders

[14]

like a steam radiator. He is anywhere from six to nine feet tall, and he looks like an Italian-opera villain."

"I know him," said Wallace. "And I don't know anything good about him or any of the other Bemises. He's the worst of a rotten lot. What about him?"

" I asked Cleppy what his uncle was doing down there among the rocks. Cleppy told me Tully Bemis was hunting for 'the treasure.' He said Tully puts in all his spare time doing that. I thought it was a joke. I asked him what 'the treasure' was. He said he had supposed everyone knew about the treasure. He said it had been hidden there, 'more'n a billion years ago, by Auntie Groot's granther and a coupla other furriner folks.'

"From all I could gather from Cleppy, it has become a sort of tradition among the mountaineers that some 'furriner folks' once buried some kind of treasure among the Ramapo Mountains. The Jackson Whites have gotten to believe it is their own—if ever they can find it. Cleppy told me Tully has thrashed every other mountaineer he caught looking for it and that he means to get it all for himself. Cleppy says his uncle has been hunting for it, off and on, all his life. The whole story sounded so silly that I supposed Tully was just grubbing for herbs or roots among the rocks and that Cleppy made up the treasure tale on the spur of the minute to impress me. But after that letter you've just read——"

"Did Tully see you watching him?"

"No. Cleppy hurried me on and he spoke in a whisper while he told me about it. He is in mortal fear of Tully. All of them seem to be. He said Tully would 'whale the

[15]

daylights outen him if he cotched him a-peekin' when he was treasurin'.' "

"It's odd, all around," mused Bladen, hoisting his angular body from his chair. "I suppose every wild mountain region has its treasure traditions that range all the way from some old miser burying a pot of silver dollars to a jewel chest of Captain Kidd's. But these Ramapo Mountains aren't like any other place I ever wandered through. The people up there are as unusual as the geological specimens I run across on my rambles into the rock summits."

"Unusual?" sniffed Wallace. "I'd call 'em just plain ornery. Meaner'n pussley."

"They aren't like any other mountaineers I ever met," pursued Bladen. "Their language, for one thing. Most of them say 'housen' and 'shoon,' for 'houses' and 'shoes.' That is pure early English. I wonder how they ever got it, out here in the north Jersey wilds. They have other queer forms of speech, too, and a scatter of Holland Dutch words. Then they have the furtive ways of savages and some of them live more like animals than humans. It's no business of mine, Miss Gates, but you are taking chances, going to and fro among them. I've heard they horse-whipped one settlement worker and chased her all the way to the valley. They——"

"Perhaps she didn't go at her work in quite the right way," suggested Sibyl. "Perhaps she didn't try to win their friendship or their confidence. It is a tedious uphill work. But I do think I'm making progress."

"I wish you were making it down here in the safe valley, instead of up there," said Bruce Hardin, worriedly. "Bladen is right. You're taking chances. I wish you wouldn't. Can't one of us go up with you to the school in the mornings and escort you back in the afternoons? I'd——"

"You'd lose two unsparable hours from work," she finished gayly, "and you'd get to hating me for stealing your time. Besides, if they thought I didn't trust them, I'd lose what little hold I've gained over them."

"Then," went on Bladen, blinking at the yellowed letter through his horn spectacles, "you spoke of Cleppy Bemis referring to 'Auntie Groot.' Twice, I've gone as far as her shack, on my geological jaunts. She is the oldest-looking creature I ever set eyes on. The oldest and the oddest. A man down at Oakland told me she is supposed to be fully a hundred years old. He says she was an elderly woman when his own grandfather was a lad. And she is still as spry as a cat. I stopped at her door once, out of curiosity, to see what sort of a den she lived in. She came running out with a kettle of boiling water and threatened to scald me to death if I didn't stop pestering her. She may very well be the granddaughter of the Hessian, Groot. If he lived to any sort of old age, she may even remember him. Some day I mean to ask her."

"Better wear a scald-proof raincoat when you do," suggested Bruce. "But you're right about her being as old as the hills. My father told me she was 'old Auntie Groot' when he was a kid. He said she is quarter Indian. But he doesn't seem to have known about the Hessian part of her ancestry. I can imagine one of the three Hessian soldiers, as an old man, getting drunk and babbling vaguely to his Afro-Indian wife about a wonderful treasure he and his comrades had buried somewhere among the hills. Of course he wouldn't have told her where it was buried. If he had,

[17]

there would be no tradition about it now. It would have been looted by her or by her kin, and the whole thing would have been forgotten by this time. No, probably he told her it was somewhere and he didn't say where. Then she told some one else, and the tradition grew. That is how such things start in a community."

"Well," said Ethan Wallace, "the rain is holding up. And that reminds me there's a mine of treasure, in the shape of my own farm, waiting to be dug. I want to arrange with you about that tractor, and then I'll be off. The best treasure-digger for both of us, right now, is the tractor we're going shares on. How about it?"

CHAPTER

2

EARLY on Monday morning Sibyl Gates set off, up the mountain trail for the shack which her benevolent society had converted into a makeshift schoolhouse. An hour later Horace Bladen set out, up the same trail.

The girl had carried a bag of books and school exercises. Bladen swung over his shoulder a battered satchel for geological specimens. In his belt was tucked his equally battered little geological hammer. He was off for one of his tours of pottering among the rock-sides of the myriad gorges and gullies which lace the Ramapos—tours whose geological results he was compiling for a forthcoming book.

Both Sibyl and Bladen, this day, were destined to encounter adventures far out of the uneventful line of work they had planned.

In a little while Bladen was busily tapping away at rocks and squinting at chipped specimens through his magnifying glass and pouring drops of ill-smelling acid on inoffensive bits of stone. He was oblivious of everything but his professional hobby.

He had rare scope for it, up there. New Jersey—near Port Jervis and at Cape May, respectively—is said to contain the oldest and the newest forms of rock formation on earth, thus seeming to imply that these two extremes of the state are among the most ancient and most newly made parts of the earth.

Sibyl, on the contrary, spent the next five hours in the uninspiring task of trying to infuse modern education into the brains of degenerate and inbred semi-savage mountaineer children. Her vigorous youth and her enthusiasm alone kept her from dire discouragement at the slowness of her pupils to absorb even the simplest forms of teaching.

To-day, as she was on her way homeward, once more crossing the ridge behind Bear Swamp, she skirted the edge of one of the smaller Jackson White settlements—a huddle of five huts, two of which were formed by nailing a harlequin pattern of rotting boards in front of the mouths of natural caves at a low cliff base. In front of one of these converted caves stood three men, evidently waiting for her.

As she drew near, the trio slouched forward to meet her. She recognized them as the Shively brothers, two of whom had children among her pupils.

"Say, woman!" Roan Shively, the most slovenly of the three, hailed her, barring her path, "I'm taking my kid outen your crazy school. Her and you made me lose three dollars and a coupla foxen skins, between you. You ain't fitten to teach nothing. Likewise I want back the cash and the value of the skins you made me lose. I whaled her 'most to death. And if you don't pay up, I'll whale you, too."

As he spoke he unbuckled the decaying bit of harness strap which served him as a belt, and swung it experimentally around his head. Sibyl stared at him in amaze. But he was not joking. Tales came back to her startled memory of the corporal punishment these Jackson Whites sometimes inflicted on their women; whom they punished as relentlessly, for trivial derelictions, as they punished their lean black mongrel hounds.

"You told my kid about this feller, C'lumbus," went on Roan, in hot accusal, "the man that invented the United States. You told her he come here in a boat, from a place called Spain. She told me about it. I figgered there wasn't many folks know that. So I aimed to win a bet on it. Moshe Wyble is always a-disagreeing with everyone and offering to bet he's right. So I betten with him that C'lumbus come here from this Spain place. He didn't say a thing. But that night he goes down to Oakland and sees the schoolmaster there.

"Next day he bets me C'lumbus didn't come from Spain. He bets me three dollars and those foxen skins. He says he'll leave it to Poke Blarcom to decide, Poke having wasted a passel of time in learning to read. We go to Poke, and Wyble shows him a printed book the schoolmaster loans him. And it says in that book that C'lumbus comes here from Yurrup. Not from Spain at all. From Yurrup. It says so in that book. Poke he reads it to us. And what a book says is true, has got to be true. So I losen my bet. And

[21]

it's your fault and my kid's. More your'n than her'n. 'Cause you learned her wrong. And you'll pay me for what I lost through my taking your word."

Sibyl struggled with a desire to laugh. But she kept her face straight and her voice steady as she tried to explain to the irate man his blunder. She might as well have talked to the rock-side behind her. Roan's face grew blacker and a cunning look came into his small eyes. Evidently he thought she was trying to enmesh him in a tangle of long words.

The information in the schoolmaster's book was sufficient for him. Print was proof positive. Sibyl had deceived him and made him lose money. One way or another she must make good on his heavy losses—either in cash or in a belting. He pointed this out to her with increasing vehemence, his onlooking brethren nodding grave approval of his denunciation.

Sibyl's wontedly sweet temper began to fray under the storm of threatening abuse. In Shively's first pause for breath she said, indignantly:

"If you can't understand that Spain is part of Europe, I can't say anything more to make you understand. As for my paying you for your silly bet, I shall do nothing of the sort. It is absurd to expect such a thing. It was brutal of you to whip poor little Manthy for your own illiteracy. I shan't pay you a cent. Please stand out of my way!"

She made as if to move on. As by concerted action, the three men closed silently in upon her.

After her first startled moment, Sibyl Gates had experienced no fear at her sudden and grotesque predicament.

She did not belong to the age wherein women used to feel they must be sheltered from all contact with the world. She had the nerve and the experience to meet life's crises calmly.

A sense of humor had carried her through black days in a nursing unit in northern France, when one must laugh or go mad. It had carried her through a score of dangers and of vicissitudes.

It was this steady nerve and keen humor-sense that had come to her aid when Shively and his brothers confronted her so threateningly.

Her brief nervousness as to her own predicament merged into a healthy desire to laugh when Roan Shively made known his weird complaint against her.

But the man's ugly insistence roused her indignation; as did his sinister gesture with the heavy-buckled belt.

All at once she realized she was in real peril.

These men would not kill her. They were not of the killer type. None of the Jackson Whites were, with the grim exception of their overlord, Tully Bemis.

But they were surlily determined to punish her—to "take it out of her hide"—for Roan's unfortunate bet.

It was wholly natural to them to revenge any loss or injury by thrashing unmercifully its author, if such victim chanced to be within reach and not too strong to turn the tables on the avenger. To them, the brutal beating of a woman seemed no worse offense than would the spanking of an unruly child.

This woman had made Roan lose money. She refused to make good the loss. Wherefore, by the natural law of the mountaineers, she must be beaten half to death by way of penance and to discourage other women from such tendencies.

Added to this was the innate hatred of a Jackson White for all intruders into the unsanctified sanctity of his community life.

Sibyl had tried to teach their children silly things like reading and writing, such as their parents had scorned. She was even coaxing their women to do highfalutin stunts like scrubbing the friendly dirt from their cabin floors and to plant useless weeds like geraniums and asters in their dooryards and to scald clean their babies' crusted milk bottles and the like.

The mountaineers had viewed all this with a growing sullen resentment. Had the girl gone about her Herculean duties in a less clever and tactful way, she would long since have shared the fate of her predecessor, who had been chased back to civilization with threats of a ducking in Rotten Pond.

Now that she had scraped raw their one tender spot— their love for such few dollars as they were able to get hold of—the climax had come. A beating, whose scars and hideous memory she should carry to her grave, was due her.

Roan was there to perform this task with eager vehemence. With his swung belt buckle before now he had inflicted almost as fearsome havoc on quivering human flesh as most men could hope to do with an ax. He was a famed expert in the line of belt-flailing.

Sibyl glanced about her. Behind was the low cliff into whose side the Shively cave-cabin was built. In front was Roan Shively, with his two brothers on either side to bar any effort to bolt past the executioner. They were closing furtively in upon her.

"Put down that belt, Shively!" she commanded, steadying her voice and looking him squarely in the eye. "Put down that belt, I say, and let me go by."

At the quiet authority in her look and tone the man hesitated for an instant, but only for an instant. He shook off the brief dominance of her will; as he and his sort shake off the weakness of the chills-and-fever which dogs them from birth to grave.

He was a man. This was only a woman. A stuck-up outlander, at that.

"I aim to get the value of that three dollars and them foxen-skins," he said, making the belt whistle in the air. "And likewise I aim to learn you not to come pestering around here again."

With his last word, he shifted the arc of the swinging and singing belt and brought its buckle end down with a vicious slash at her slender shoulders.

Instinctively Sibyl sprang back with the swiftness of light. The spring brought her against the cliffside, but it made the mountaineer's blow fall short by a matter of three inches.

Down whizzed the strap, missing its mark and moving with too much momentum to be checked in midair. The metal buckle smote resoundingly against Shively's own bare ankle bone, the impact wringing from him a howl of anguish.

He was better geared for inflicting pain than for enduring it.

The stinging hurt roused him to blind fury. Striding forward, he towered above the girl as she shrank with her back against the cliff's low wall. In air flew the buckle again, this time with double force.

"Hands up, please!" called a quiet voice just above the group. This is ever an order which calls for notice, if not for obedience. At sound of it Roan Shively checked his downward sweep of the strap and stared blankly about. The voice had been calm, even light, but under its lightness ran a note of something vaguely deadly.

The three men centered their roaming gaze on the cliff just above them—the cliff against whose side Sibyl's young body was pressing for protection.

At the edge of the trail that crowned the tiny precipice Horace Bladen was standing. Almost always he returned homeward by this path. For once he had chanced to arrive at the right spot at the right time.

He stood, his mild blue eyes blinking down at the scene through his horn spectacles, his lean face flushed but expressionless. In one hand he was carrying his bag of rock specimens.

The other arm was outstretched toward Roan Shively. In its hand glittered evilly a shiny weapon whose muzzle covered the mountaineer. Silhouetted black against a glare of afternoon sunlight stood the geologist, rigid, tensely murderous.

"Hands up!" he repeated, a tinge of impatience now in his light voice.

"*Up!* All three of you!"

The glittering muzzle menaced the heads of the trio of brethren in turn. Under its threat, one after another of them lifted sulkily a pair of unwashed hands.

"That's better," mildly approved Bladen. "Now then,

all three of you keep your arms up, and—Drop that strap, Roan! *Drop* it!"

He spoke as if giving an order to a disobedient dog. The buckled strap flopped to the ground.

"Now move backward, all three of you," went on the geologist. "Hands still up, unless you're looking for more trouble than you can carry among you. Back up to that door."

The open doorways of the cliffside shacks were full of white and terrified faces. Two women and a half-dozen children of Roan's household were peering out on the scene. As the back-shuffling trio neared the opening of Roan's hovel the watchers scattered.

"Keep on backing!" commanded Bladen, his weapon-muzzle never for a moment straying from one or another of the men. "Keep close together there!" as Roan sheered somewhat away from his fellows in an effort to dodge behind a dooryard boulder.

"Now into the hut with you, one after the other. One of you children shut the door after the last of them."

Swearing thickly, mumbling and snarling like cowed wild animals, the three brothers shuffled clumsily indoors, their hands still waveringly aloft. A little girl, clad only in a burlap bag, tremblingly pushed shut the creaky portal after them, at Bladen's order.

Horace came down the few yards of steep cliff path.

"Miss Gates," he said, "will you please go ahead as fast as you can? I'll probably catch up with you before you get home. Just now I am going to stay till you get away clear. There is always a chance that our friends may come out with a gun, as soon as our backs are turned. I want to stay

[27]

here to welcome the first of them who puts his nose outside that door."

He spoke clearly, raising his weak voice to be heard in the hovel. A jumbled muttering from within showed his words had carried.

"But you?" queried the frightened girl. "Aren't you in danger from——?"

He laughed in tolerant contempt at the idea.

"Run on, please," he urged. "I shan't let them see my back till I'm out of shotgun range. Besides—well, even a moron mountaineer would be too sane to shoot me, with you gone ahead. You'd be a witness that would send all three of them to the electric chair. They know that much. Go ahead, please."

Reluctantly Sibyl moved on. Presently a turn of the rocky path shut her from sight. On she went, ashamed of herself for obeying, her ears straining for sound of a shot.

But only the soft silences of the spring afternoon were about her. Gathering assurance, she continued on her way.

Hitherto she had regarded Horace as a mildly uninteresting scientist, and she had wondered at Bruce Hardin's liking for so uninspiring a man. Now, for the first time, she could understand the friendship between the two men.

The health-broken geologist who puttered about the farm, doing light jobs, and whose recreation hours were spent in chipping and classifying bits of stone, seemed suddenly transformed into a paladin of valor, a rescuer of distressed womanhood. The rôle fitted him as ill as might Manthy Shively's single potato-sack garment.

At the foot of the mountain, where a bridge spans the narrow Ramapo, the girl paused. There she waited. There, two minutes later, she caught the clump of Horace Bladen's hiking boots.

Presently Bladen appeared around the bend of the trail. He beamed reassuringly at her from behind his spectacles.

"I'm horribly sorry you had such a fright, Miss Gates!" he hailed as he drew near. "If only I had been able to get there just one minute sooner! But then after I did arrive I had to waste still more time, getting the light behind me."

"The light behind you?" she repeated, puzzled.

"Yes," he made sheepish excuse. "You see, if they had had a fair look at me it would have been all off. But I counted on their squinting up to where I stood with the sun right at my back. And they did."

"I—I don't understand," she faltered, bewildered at the inexplicable things he was saying in his precise schoolmaster diction. "Besides, I haven't even thanked you, Mr. Bladen!" she broke off. "It is abominably ungrateful in me. But, honestly, I'm *not* ungrateful! *Truly*, I'm not. I do thank you with all my heart. It was—it was splendid of you. If it hadn't been for you——"

Her words of gratitude broke off in an involuntary shudder as she recalled the whistling swish of the strap above her head.

"Oh!" she cried, in sudden revulsion. "I could almost wish you really *had* shot him."

"I wished so, too," agreed Bladen. "And if I could have done it I'm afraid I should. But, you see, I never carry a pistol. I hated to do it, even in the war. And this thing couldn't very well go off. That's why I stood with my back to the sun."

As he spoke he drew forth the weapon wherewith he had

[29]

menaced the Shivelys. He held it as before, the sunlight glinting from its metal surface. But now, at close quarters, Sibyl could see what it was.

It was Bladen's little steel-handled geological hammer.

He was holding it by the head. The well-worn handle shone brightly in the sun. Its blackened end, even now, bore some likeness to the muzzle of a pistol.

Sibyl looked wide-eyed at the thing for a moment. Then, in spite of herself, she burst into hysterical laughter.

This puny convalescent, with a futile little chipping-hammer, had held up and cowed three ruffians any one of whom could have killed him at a blow.

The idea smote upon the girl's sense of the ridiculous. Try as she would she could not force back her laughter. Bladen gazed at her in mild reproof.

"It isn't my fault there isn't anything of the hero about me," he said, humbly. "There never was. But the main thing is that I was lucky enough to save you from ill-treatment. Maybe that's of more practical use than being a hero. Besides," he defended himself, "you'll notice I never told them it was a pistol. So it wasn't a lie. I just let them believe what they wanted to believe. I didn't say it was a pistol. I didn't say I'd shoot them. I took pains not to say so. I don't think I've done anything actually dishonorable in fooling them. Do you?"

He asked the question solicitously. But at once his solicitation increased tenfold, for, under his apologetic words her laughter had turned unexpectedly into uncontrolled weeping.

"Oh, I'm so sorry!" he cried. "I ought to have known

the shock had been too much for you. Here I've gone on babbling to you, when you ought to have hurried home and gone to bed! I——"

"No!" she sobbed, catching at his arm, as he would have moved on. "*No!* It isn't that. Oh, I'm ashamed to be so babyish as to cry! But when I heard you talk about not being a hero, I—all of a sudden I—oh, you don't even see how glorious you are! That's the pitiful part of it. A hero? Why, can't you understand you've done something a million times more heroic than if you really had been armed? Can't you see that?"

"Nonsense!"

"It wouldn't have taken much courage to face those unarmed men with a real pistol. But it took a world of heroism to do it when you staked everything on their not knowing you weren't armed. They could have killed you. And you knew it. Yet you were as cool as if you had a machine-gun company behind you. Can't you see—? Oh, I'm talking like a crazy school-girl! And I can't make you understand how fine you are. But I want you to know I'll never forget it and that I'll never stop being grateful to——"

"No! *Please*, no!" he implored, pink and stuttering with embarrassment. "I'm not any of those grand-opera things you've been calling me. And I won't have you being grateful to me, either. We always end up by loathing the people we have to be grateful to, and I'd hate to have you loathe me, Miss Gates. Now, if you've had your cry out, suppose we walk on home."

"I—I——"

"I want to show you something," he cut her short as he

fumbled in his disreputable bag. "I blundered on a grand specimen to-day. I didn't know there was any trace of it this side of the Hartz Mountains. Just a freak outcrop, of course, but none the less interesting for that. See."

He held out a crumbly fragment of rock.

"Pyrargyrite," he said. "But see that vein in it. That is fair-grade antimony. Think of that! *Antimony!* Did you ever hear of such a thing? Up here in the north Jersey hinterland, too! I shall be called a gross falsifier when I tell of that in my book. But what a sensation it will make!"

She looked up into his glowing eyes, in amaze. The thrill of his worthless geological find had already wiped from his memory the fact that he had so recently faced death for her sake. With a sigh, Sibyl gave up all hope of understanding him or of making him understand himself.

Bruce Hardin had come in from a back-breaking day of corn-planting. He was on his way indoors to wash up for supper when he chanced to notice Horace and Sibyl crossing a field path from the river. Bruce paused on the farmhouse porch, waiting for Bladen to join him.

At Hardin's side was Mars, his big gold-red collie, who had come in from the rich riverside cornfields with him. Mars flung himself down heavily, panting, on the veranda. The early May day had been unseasonably hot. The collie still carried his massive winter coat. Nothing short of his absolute love for his master would have kept him out in the broiling sun in such weather. For collies suffer keenly from shadeless heat.

A human would have made excuses to dodge a day of

constant discomfort, even for the sake of being with some loved comrade. But Mars was only a dog. Thus, discomfort and danger of heat attack meant nothing to him in comparison to the joy of staying near his god.

Bruce's brows contracted ever so little as he marked the parting between Sibyl and Bladen at the spot where one fork of the path led to the Hardin house and the other to Ethan Wallace's, where the girl boarded.

It seemed to him that their handclasp was unduly long and fervent and that the girl's upraised face was alight with more than mere friendliness. Not knowing what had passed, he wondered much and worriedly at Sibyl's warmth of manner toward his chum.

He wondered still more at his own unaccountable irritation at the sight. Always, during their brief acquaintance, he had liked Sibyl. Always he had sought her society in his few hours of leisure. But he had not realized that the young teacher had grown to mean anything more to him than a pleasant friend. Even now he found it hard to analyze his own annoyance at her new manner toward Bladen.

It had been a wearying and annoying day for the farmer. The first intense heat had taken toll of his strength and his nerves. Many vexing things had happened, including the absence on a spree of his one hired man and the discovery that a bag of seed corn had gone moldy by reason of a leak in the storeroom roof.

The sight of Horace Bladen strolling homeward, unwearied and unruffled, in the late afternoon, formed too sharp a contrast with his own sweating and prickly-heated condition to add to his peace of mind.

Forgetting that Horace was still convalescing and was unfit for sustained farm labor, he resented the other's cool comfort. As Bladen came up to the steps, Bruce replied with a surly grunt to his friend's hail.

"You look as if you'd had a wakeful day," observed Bladen, glancing at his sullen and perspiring companion.

"*You* look as if you hadn't," grumbled Bruce, turning toward the open front door. "You're lucky."

"I was lucky this afternoon," assented Bladen. "For once in my twenty-nine years of life I happened to arrive in the right place at the right time."

"I saw you did," said Hardin, dryly. "I take it the 'right place' was somewhere between here and the Jackson Whites' schoolhouse."

"Yes," assented Horace. "Just above Roan Shiveley's cabin. You remember Roan, don't you? He came to work for you once, last fall, and stayed half a day. You were missing things around the farm for a week afterward. By the way, Sibyl Gates ought not to be allowed to go around alone in those mountains. It's unsafe."

"So I told her," answered Bruce, ungraciously. "And so Wallace told her. And so you told her. And so half the neighborhood has told her. But I can't see that it is any special business of yours any more than of mine or——"

"If it hadn't been any special business of mine, this afternoon," said Bladen, unruffled by his friend's grumpiness, "she'd have been one-hundred-per-cent eligible for the accident ward of the Paterson General Hospital by this time. That's what I meant when I said I was lucky."

"What are you talking about?" demanded Hardin, turning back from the doorway. "If it's a joke——"

[34]

"It is," answered Horace. "And the joke is on Roan Shively."

"What has Shively got to do with it?" asked the perplexed Bruce, his curiosity roused by the other's carelessly spoken cryptic words.

Concisely, modestly, with no shadow of excitement or self-applause, Bladen told him what had happened.

Bruce listened, his tanned face reddening darkly with wrath. As Bladen finished, Hardin caught him by the hand with a pressure that hurt.

"Horace," he said, contritely, "I'm all sorts of a swine to have been grouchy with you. Lord! but you came through like a he-one! Bluffed those three big toughs with that measly little hammer! And I thought I'd had a stiffer day than you had! I——"

He paused. Then the angry red deepened in his face and the veins on his forehead stood out.

"The mangy brutes!" he blazed. "And from what I know of them, they'd have done as Roan threatened. You're right about saying she ought not to set foot among the mountains again. She mustn't."

"But she will. She told me so. I begged her not to. But she says she isn't frightened. I can't make her understand that Roan is liable to waylay her the first chance he gets, and——"

"H'm!" snarled Bruce. "Then if you couldn't make her understand it, the only thing left is to make Roan understand it. I'll be back in an hour or so. Don't wait supper for me."

At a stride he was off the veranda and heading toward the river.

"Where are you going?" asked Bladen, puzzled.

"Where would I be going?" angrily called back Hardin, over his shoulder. "If Sibyl is too pigheaded to see there is danger from Roan, then it's up to me to take the danger out of Roan. That's what I'm going to do. If there's no use in talking to her, I'll make it my business to see that there's plenty of use in talking to *him*."

"I'll come along!" cried Bladen, eagerly.

"Go back!" ordered Bruce, from halfway across the door-yard. "You've done your bit, to-day. It's up to me to do mine."

"But——"

"Do as I ask you!" commanded Bruce, his tone leaving no loophole for argument.

"But come back and get a gun or——"

Bruce Hardin laughed aloud—a laugh that was not sweet to hear. By way of reply to Horace's suggestion, he flexed his mighty arm muscles. The gesture told much to Bladen, who recalled his chum's college prowess as a boxer and at football.

Uneasy, yet obeying, Bladen seated himself on the porch and watched the big athletic figure swing across the mead-ows toward the river and the grim mountains beyond.

Yet Bruce Hardin did not go alone. At his first step Mars bounded up from the cool veranda boards where he was resting and galloped in his master's wake. Eagerly he fol-lowed Bruce, to whatever toil or adventure might be in store for them both.

Hardin patted carelessly the silken head of his collie as Mars came trotting alongside. But he had to unclench a tight fist to do it. A righteous anger was swirling hot within the young farmer as he recalled Sibyl's danger and the vagabond who had caused it. In a dazing flash he realized what she had come to mean to him.

CHAPTER

3

THE three Shively brothers lounged in regal laziness on their backs in the cluttered space in front of their cliffside hovel, watching slab-sided women make ready their evening meal.

From time to time one or another of them would grunt an order to the frightened workers to make more haste in the preparations; an order coupled with a mountaineer oath. They were unwontedly surly and profane toward their womenfolk, this evening. All three had been humiliated most grossly in these women's presence by that gun-toting outlander, Bladen. It was needful to restore their own self-esteem and the women's cringing respect by unusual show of truculence.

They lay there, muttering and mumbling to one another, foretelling the dire punishments they were going to inflict on Bladen if ever any of them should come upon him when he was not armed. Still more vehemently they dilated on the retribution which they were going to lavish upon Sibyl Gates, should she venture into the mountains again.

Thus were they salving their scratched pride when one of the tatterdemalion children grouped in the doorway sang out, shrilly:

"Some one's a-coming! Someb'dy with shoon on!"

The men sat up, their mountain-trained ears catching what Manthy's sharper hearing already had detected. A booted tread sounded springily along the path leading up-hill toward the cabin.

Not thus do the Jackson Whites stride along when cold weather or other causes enforce the wearing of boots. This was an outlander. The three men looked at one another, then they began to scramble to their feet. At the same moment Bruce Hardin rounded the cliff-edge and was in front of them.

Roan Shively had been the first of the trio to start up from the ground. His heel slipped under him on a scrap of greasy pork rind and he sat down heavily.

He got up again at once, but through no effort or volition of his own. Bruce Hardin took a single long step forward and caught the recumbent man by the shirt collar. With a sharp heave he yanked him to his feet.

Still holding him thus and without a word, he reached for Roan's belt. In one twist he unfastened it and whirled aloft its buckle end.

Before Roan could grasp his intent and before either of the two other men could interfere, Bruce brought down the belt with a vicious smash athwart Roan's shoulder.

[39]

The buckle tore its way through vest and shirt and bit deep into the grimed skin of the mountaineer's back. Roan bellowed like a calf that has stepped into a hornet nest.

He tugged and wrenched, to tear free from the grip on the back of his neck. Strong as he was, he might as well have tried to break loose from the vise of a hundred-gallon cider-press.

Down came the hurtling and hurting belt again; with double force; this time swishing murderously about his loins. His screeches awoke a million echoes from the hills and ravines around him.

Forward lurched Roan's two brothers; one of them catching up a paintless wagon spoke. Forward sprang two gaunt and jet-black dogs from before the cabin door—wolf-like mongrels of hyena ferocity. To Roan's assistance advanced these reinforcements, as an augmented howl from the victim attested to a third torturing descent of the belt buckle.

As calm and as clear-headed as ever he had been in a football crisis, Bruce viewed the oncomers. For the first time he spoke.

"Mars!" he called, imperatively, accenting his words with a fourth blow of the belt. "*Hold* 'em!"

He had no need for even this brief command. The collie had been dancing wildly around his master and Roan, venting his gay excitement by a slash that cut bone deep in the latter's thigh. He seemed to divine the onset of reinforcements almost before they moved forward.

Spinning about, he faced the two other men and the curs that pressed past them. Ruff abristle, teeth glinting, a smear of blood on his white frill, Mars confronted them.

At his swift display of eagerness, one of the brothers re-

coiled a step. The other—he who wielded the wagon spoke
—stood his ground and aimed a mighty blow at the collie.
The blow fell. But it did not reach its mark. This because
its mark had sprung aside, with the speed of light, from
under the descending stroke.

The wagon spoke hit the rocky ground with a force that
splintered it and numbed the striker's arm to the elbow.
By the time the spoke had struck ground, Mars flashed in
and drove his teeth deep into the numbed forearm. The
whole duel had not lasted three seconds, yet at its conclu-
sion the assailant was reeling back, nursing a numb and
torn arm, the fight wholly taken out of him for the time.

One of the two black dogs had been less cautious than
his fellow, which had come to a halt as the great red-gold
collie whizzed about on them and on the two men. This
braver mongrel had dived forward, wolf-like, head close to
the ground, charging for Mars's shaggy throat.

The collie's maneuver in dodging the stick and then at-
tacking the striker had made the black dog miss his aim.
Now he charged afresh. And now Mars had a second or so
in which to attend to him.

Slipping easily aside from the clumsy rush, the collie
wheeled and caught the black dog by the nape of the neck
as the cur plunged past. Pinning his enemy to the ground,
Mars shook him as though he were a giant rat. Cannily he
kept his own legs and body out of reach of the futilely
snapping jaws as he swung the mongrel savagely to and
fro in an agonizing shaking.

Now canine yells were added to human, as the shaken
cur changed Roan Shively's solo of anguish to a duet.

Never once had Bruce ceased his scientifically rapid

flailing of the belt. Roan's clothes from neck to knee hung in shreds; his body was one interlacing pattern of angry weals.

Then came an unlooked-for interruption in the fast enacted punitive drama.

The unhurt black dog still slunk, snarling and growling scared defiance, well out of reach of the red-gold devil that was shaking the life out of his litter-brother. The two Shivelys also hung back, one of them moaning and swaying in pain as he inspected his torn arm.

But some one else—fearless and efficient and pathetic—was rushing to Roan's aid.

Out from the shack, brandishing a rusty hatchet, scuttled a scarecrow wisp of a woman, lank and homely and ragged, and with thin hair flying. She was Roan Shively's wife.

Not yet thirty, she looked nearer sixty, thanks to the undernourishment and overtoil of the Jackson White women. But she came on like a Fury, to the rescue of her husband—she whose thin back still bore weals from the same belt which was now avenging her myriad beatings.

Indifferent to peril from dog or outlander, she hurtled forward. Bruce Hardin saw her coming. Into his heart seeped a twinge of utter pity for her loyalty to the brute he was beating. With a final blow he flung the shrieking Roan to the ground and threw the blood-spattered belt far into the scrubby hillside bushes.

"Mars!" he said.

At the summons, the collie gave over his congenial task of shaking the terrified black mongrel to death. Howling, the cur slunk away, seeking the nearest place of safety.

Mars ranged himself in front of his master. With head on one side and with tulip ears cocked, he surveyed the hatchet-swinging Amazon.

Had a man approached Bruce in this warlike manner, Mars would have been at his throat on sight. But a woman was different. He had a collie's queer innate sense of protectiveness toward women and little children. Here was a phase in the situation he felt was beyond his powers. From Mrs. Shively he glanced up at Hardin, in curiosity.

"The beating is over, madam," said Bruce, pleasantly. "No need to save him from me now. I'm through with him —for the present. It is up to him to say whether I'm through with him for good, or not."

The woman paused uncertainly. Through the rage mists she saw her husband writhing on the ground like some broken-backed rattlesnake. Evidently deciding that retribution could wait until she should have learned the extent of her spouse's injuries, she dropped the hatchet and plumped herself down on her knees beside the bellowing man.

The unhurt brother moved slyly forward in the direction of the fallen hatchet. The other women and the children, in the doorway, noted his action. They checked their own screams to watch avidly.

Bruce, too, observed the stealthy approach. Stooping, he picked up the hatchet as the man's hand was about to close on it. With all his might he flung it down the rocky mountain-side, after the belt.

"Now, then!" he announced crisply, "it's time to say what I came up here to say. You'll all do well to listen. For your own sakes, not for mine. And listen *carefully*."

Roan's two brothers eyed him slack-jawed. The women in the doorway faced him in dull terror. Even Roan Shively's wife paused in her dual task of soothing her husband's hurts and of squalling threats and insults at his conqueror. Before the brief lull could be broken Hardin went on, in the same incisive voice:

"Roan, you tried to thrash a woman to-day—a woman whose name you're not fit to speak. Mr. Bladen stopped you, at the point of the gun he always carries. And, by the way, he's never yet missed a shot he's fired with it. He's quick on the draw. You'll be wise to give him a wide berth.

"Well, I came up here to show you what we Ramapo Valley farmers think of a man who'd belt a woman. I've shown you. I want to tell you, on my oath, that if any man in these mountains ever so much as gives Miss Gates an ugly look again, I am coming up here to finish what I've begun. And there are plenty of others who'll come along with me, to see the job is done completely.

"She is going to keep on with her work up here, and she is going to do it in perfect safety. If she is bothered in any way, there won't be a whole inch of uncut skin on the man who is to blame, and what is left of him will go to jail for ten years. That's all. I think you'll remember."

He turned his back on them, not even doing them the honor to look over his shoulder to see if any were pursuing.

Mars, at a snap of Hardin's fingers, trotted gayly on ahead, leading the way down the path. The Jackson Whites moved not, nor spoke, as they stared after them.

But as he disappeared around the end of the cliff Mrs. Shively leaped up and ran into the house. Running out again with a rusty double-barreled gun in her arms, she thrust it into her husband's convulsive grasp.

"Roan!" she shrilled, venomously. "Arter him. *Git* him!"

Bruce Hardin thought he knew Jackson White nature as well as it is given to any normal man to know it. He had roamed these mountains as a boy, as had his ancestors before him. He had inherited these ancestors' thorough contempt for the degenerate mountaineers.

Angry as he had been, his punitive expedition had been made with shrewd purpose. He knew if he could frighten the Shivelys badly enough, they would not dare molest Sibyl on her future trips to the mountains.

He knew that the tale of Roan's merciless beating would be all over the Ramapos inside of twenty-four hours, and that it would serve as a sharp deterrent to any further attempts against Sibyl among the folk who strew the tumble of hills from Suffern to Pompton.

He had gone up to the Shively hovel with a set purpose. That purpose he had fulfilled. He believed this was the end of the incident. He had insured Sibyl's safety at mountaineer hands. Concerning his own safety he did not so much as think.

"Mars," he addressed the gold-red collie that trotted down the steeply winding path just ahead of him, between undergrowth and boulders—"Mars, you're a mighty good pal to have along in a pinch. You're all right, old friend."

Like many semi-lonely men, Bruce had gotten into the way of talking to this collie chum of his as to a fellow-human. Mars rejoiced always in this friendly custom of his master's. The dog did not understand one word in ten, of

[45]

course, but he gathered much from the various tones Hardin employed in speaking to him. For this is the way of a collie.

Now, hearing his name spoken and realizing from Bruce's voice that he was being praised, the dog wheeled about to thrust his nose caressingly into the man's hand.

The path was steep and pebbly. The dog made so quick a turn that his furry body was right athwart the path and on a level with Hardin's knees. Bruce was moving at a fast gait. This sudden obstacle made him come to so abrupt a halt in order not to step on the collie, that his carelessly maintained balance was overthrown.

Hardin pitched forward before he could catch himself, landing on all-fours in the path, barking his palms against its stones. He and Mars were tangled momentarily in a conglomerate mass of arms and legs.

As though his fall were a signal, the sweet sunset silences were shattered by the roar of a gun. Two barrels were fired in immediate succession.

Above the prostrate Bruce's head sang a handful of buckshot, tearing its way through the witch-hazel thicket directly in front of him. The man's fall was providentially well timed. Evidently it had occurred at the same instant that the gunner pulled trigger.

Hardin clambered to his feet, whirling about to see whence the shots had come. The uphill patch behind him was void of life. But just at a turn of it a hazy puff of disintegrating whitish smoke hung in the windless air.

At the reports Mars had spun about. Now he charged up the hill.

"Back here!" called Hardin. "Heel! You're too good a mark, if he's still hiding there. *Heel!*"

At the command Mars dropped reluctantly behind his master. Bruce, heedless of possible danger to himself, was scrambling up the steep path at top speed, in the direction whence the firing had come.

Well did he understand the meaning of the attack, and he was annoyed with himself for underestimating so vaingloriously the possible results of his treatment of Roan Shively.

In his heart blazed hot wrath at the attempted murder. Later, there would be time to think of the gruesome sound made by the double charge of buckshot as it had whistled over his fallen body and crashed into the hazel copse. Just now his one thought was to punish the cowardly attempt.

With no caution he ran up the path and around its bend. No one was in sight. Mars at his heels, he raced onward until he came out at the little cluttered clearing in front of Shively's cliff hut.

The clearing was empty. The crazy door stood ajar. The hovel's dirty interior was destitute of human life. The surrounding huts were empty.

With all their hereditary mountaineer craftiness, the household had scattered and had taken cover at first sound of Hardin's running footsteps far down the path.

Bruce had too much sense and too much experience to try to seek out the fugitives. As wisely try, unaided, to locate the members of a scurrying family of rabbits or a scatter of partridges.

True, Mars could have scented out the hiding-place of

[47]

one or more of the refugees for him. But the chances were ten to one against his finding Roan, among that ruck of women and children. Roan was certain to have fled first and fastest, as soon as he had noted the failure of his shots.

Bruce Hardin stood for an instant in perplexity. Then from his trousers pocket he exhumed a crumpled envelope and a pencil stub. On the back of the envelope he scrawled, in printed letters:

I shall telephone the sheriff of Bergen County, to-night. If I am ever found dead or if my house or ricks are burned, he will bring a posse up here and land you all in jail for life.

"There, Mars," commented Hardin, as he and the collie set forth once more down the mountain after he had pinned the envelope to the open door, "they'll take that note around till they find some one who can read it to them. They'll think it's gospel truth because it's in print. We've nothing more to worry about from them. These poor white trash aren't killers by nature. If Roan hadn't been crazy with pain, he'd never have had the nerve to try it. He won't try again. Just the same, you'll stay on guard outside to-night, Mars, on the chance they may take a whirl at incendiarism before they find some one who can read."

The collie wagged his plumed tail appreciatively at the mention of his name, but forbore to stand across the narrow path again to listen to the harangue. His flesh was still bruised from Bruce's fortunate tumble over him.

As the man and the dog crossed the last meadow between the Hardin homestead and the river, Bruce saw three people watching them from the porch. The three

[48]

came forward to meet him as he entered the dooryard.

Sibyl had told the story of her adventure to Ethan Wallace, who had insisted worriedly on coming over at once to the Hardin house to talk it over with Bruce and Bladen, and to enlist their aid in helping him persuade the girl from going back next day to her perilous labors among the Jackson Whites.

Sore against his wish, Sibyl had come with him, to offset his possible eloquence. Horace had scarcely had time to tell them of Hardin's jaunt into the mountains when Bruce and Mars came into view on the way back. Anxious at his long absence, they trooped forth to meet him.

"All right?" sung out Ethan Wallace as they came within call.

"All right!" answered Bruce, reassuringly.

"Just before we came over here I thought I heard a gunshot or maybe a couple of gunshots, back somewheres in the mountains," went on Wallace. "They weren't shooting you up any, were they?"

"Not so you'd notice it," laughed Bruce in elaborate unconcern. "Probably you heard the six-o'clock blasts at the stonecrusher down in Bloomingdale. When the wind is right, they sound a lot like far-off firing. Did you and Miss Gates come over for supper? If you did, where's Mrs. Wallace?"

"Ma is getting supper at home, where teacher and I ought to be right now," said Wallace. "We're letting supper get cold over there. And the wife's temper isn't a whole heap the better for her good suppers being let spoil by folks' lateness. But I wanted to see if I could get you boys to coax teacher to cut out that silly teaching stunt of hers. After

[49]

what she's just told me, I figger it isn't anyways safe for her to—"

"Oh, it's safe enough!" replied Bruce, confidently. "I think I can guarantee nobody is going to bother her, up there, after this. I've been talking to Roan Shively and his tribe. I've talked to them like a stage father. I've made them see reason. Miss Gates, you'll be safe enough, next time you go back. Just the same, Wallace is right about its being foolish in you to go. You can't hammer decency and education into those roustabouts' brains, if you try a lifetime. You couldn't do it by an operation on their skulls. Why not call it a day and quit?"

"No," said Sibyl, very quietly but very determinedly.

As she spoke her keen glance was taking in the raw surfaces of Bruce's palms and the smears of drying blood on Mars's white throat frill. She could not read aright these signs of conflict. But they spelled something more drastic than the mere fatherly talk Bruce claimed to have had with the Shivelys.

Into her soft gray eyes and into her heart crept a tinge of admiration for this unruffled athlete who was seeking to spare her feelings by withholding the story of his battle in her behalf.

For his palms and the dog's frill, almost as much as a queer flash of feminine intuition, told her that a battle had been waged and that he had fought it for her future safety as well as to avenge the affront of that afternoon.

Then, shaking off the unwonted thrill that swept through her, she made further answer in a matter-of-fact way:

"I don't see why I should stop my work there just because a man happened to treat me as if I was one of his own wom-

[50]

ankind; especially since Mr. Hardin says it won't happen again. Besides, it's my livelihood, you know. Summer is coming on. If I should give this up, I couldn't expect to get another position anywhere as a teacher till September. No, I'm going back to-morrow, as usual. And I thank you ever and ever so much, Mr. Hardin, for preaching the gospel of decency to them, as you say you did. Almost as much as I thank Mr. Bladen for his gorgeous hold-up tactics this afternoon."

To quell the unbidden stir at her heart she spoke the words of gratitude more coldly than she intended to, her sweet voice warming only as she referred to Bladen's part in the affair. Once more, against his will, Bruce's forehead contracted into a shadow of a frown.

At once he banished the jealous twinge, and when he spoke it was with no trace of other feeling than polite solicitude.

"Just the same," he said, "if it will keep you from being nervous, I can lend you dad's little derringer pistol. I have it upstairs somewhere. For close quarters the old-time derringer has never been surpassed by any modern gun. It is small enough to go easily into your pocket. And—"

Her laugh cut short the offer.

"No, thanks," she said. "I wouldn't know what to do with it. And in any time of need I'm sure I'd forget I had it with me. I never shot a pistol and I don't know how. Thanks, just the same."

"Then there's a present you can't well refuse," insisted Hardin. "Something a good deal more formidable than a pistol. You're the only person on earth that Mars has ever consented to make real friends with, except me. And you

[51]

told me once that you liked him better than any other dog you'd seen."

"I—"

"I want you to take Mars as a gift from me," said Bruce, earnestly. "I want you to accept him as a present and as a safeguard. Take him with you, back and forth, on your trips to school. He'll be the finest protection in the world for you. *Please* do!"

He spoke with eagerness, the more so since he loved the great collie as hitherto he had loved no human friend. To lose Mars's hourly companionship was something he dared not let himself think about, lest he falter in his offer. Nothing but his new-born love for the girl would have made him consent to sacrifice his ownership of the wise and fearless dog he had bred and reared.

Sibyl Gates's clear gray eyes read his thoughts to the very soul. A sudden mist sprang into these eyes of hers at thought of what he was offering to give up for her sake.

CHAPTER

4

THE two men stared at Bruce agape. Both knew his love for the collie and the tremendous volume of farm work Mars was able to do for his master, in the way of herding and driving flocks and in guarding the homestead. Unnoticed by Bruce, old Wallace and Bladen exchanged a sharp glance. Ethan was about to speak, but Sibyl forestalled him.

"I think," she said, slowly—"I think that is the most wonderful offer you or any man could make. I shall never forget it. But you ought to know I can't accept it."

"But I—"

"Don't you see," she pursued, "Mars would never really be my dog, if you should give him to me a million times over. He'd always be your dog, just as he is now. He is yours not because you own him, but because he has chosen

[53]

you as his god. It wouldn't matter whom you gave him to or sold him to. He'd always be yours, just the same. He'd pine if he was away from you. The first chance he got he'd come flying back to you, wherever he was. No, thanks. It's beautiful of you. But I can't take him."

"I'm sure he'd be happy with you," urged Bruce, ashamed of his own relief at her refusal. "Besides—"

"Besides," she mocked, "you know what I just said about him is true. Don't let's—"

"Then," he begged, "let's compromise on the offer. And you'll have to do this, whether you want to or not. Because I'm going to give him the order every day, and he'll obey it."

"What order?" she asked, perplexed.

"Every morning when you set out for the mountains," he explained, "I'm going to send Mars along with you. I'm going to tell him to stay with you till you come back. He'll mind me. And he'll understand he is to guard you. Now that's what I'm going to do, whether you want me to or not."

"I *do* want you to," she replied, gratefully. "I'd like it above all things. Not that I need a guard. But—it's so hideously lonely up there—lonelier than in a desert—as lonely as being the only sane person in an asylum for violent lunatics. Mars will be glorious company for me. And by contrast to most of the Jackson Whites he will be a Daniel Webster for wisdom and companionship. Thank you, more than I can say. I'll stop by for him when I start to-morrow morning, and I'll bring him back to you, safe and sound, in the afternoon. I—"

"Mary's little lamb wasn't a patch on what that big

red collie will stir up by going to school," suggested Wallace. "I can figger how Sibyl will make those idjit kids behave by saying she'll sic him on to them if they don't."

"I shan't do anything of the sort," declared Sibyl. "But there ought to be a good dog in every school. I think the example of a splendid collie like Mars will have a fine effect on the children's behavior."

"It will, on the behavior of their dads, anyhow," agreed Wallace. "Now, let's—"

"It is so strange," murmured Sibyl, unhearing, her gaze fixed on the sunset-lit mountain walls rising soft and majestic like a pile of dark emerald velvet against the fireglow of the spring sunset. "It is so strange that such people should live there! Our darling Ramapo Mountains! To me they're the dearest part of all the world. They seem like benignant giants keeping watch over this valley as if they loved it. Every inch of them is beautiful, with their summits and gorges and hidden fire-blue lakes and their enchanted forests. They—they seem to lay a golden spell on one's spirit.

"The first time I ever saw them I fell under their magic. It seemed to me that such a mountain paradise must be inhabited by demigods and by valkyrs and nymphs and fauns and all the sublime and beauty-loving folk in the mythologies. Then, when I explored them, I found—the Jackson Whites! It's like Bishop Heber's old missionary hymn that says Ceylon is a place 'where every prospect pleases and only man is vile'! Those mountains are so wonderful and wild—"

"They aren't anywhere so wild as Mrs. W. is going to be if we stay gabbling here while her good supper gets burned to a cinder," interrupted Wallace, stifling a yawn. "Let's be traipsing home, young lady."

Having been born and raised in the shadow of the mystically beautiful mountain wall, the farmer was immune to its glories. But a lifetime of usage had never yet rendered him immune to the bliss of a supper of viscid hot spare-ribs and cabbage, such as he knew was now awaiting the girl and himself in his farmhouse kitchen.

Homeward fared Wallace and his young boarder. Bruce watched them go, his mind still marveling confusedly at this new feeling toward Sibyl that had leaped unasked into his life. Bladen broke in on his companion's brooding with the query:

"You did have a fight up there, didn't you? I thought those two reports sounded too near to come all the way from Bloomingdale. I was going to get your rifle and start up there on a rescue expedition, only, I couldn't find where you keep it. I would have come up without it, and brought Wallace along, only, just as I stopped hunting for the rifle and just as he and Miss Gates came over here, I saw you crossing the bridge down below there and I knew you must be all right. What happened? Was it a good fight?"

"It wasn't any fight at all," answered Bruce. "I belted Roan Shively and I told him what would happen if Miss Gates was pestered again. Some of the others tried to horn in, but good old Mars stood them off. Then, when I had made my talk, I started home."

"You—?"

"Some one—probably Roan—tried to speed me on my way with a handful of buckshot. Mars had just tripped me up and the shot went over my head. I went back to expostulate, but they had all cleared out, so I left a notice tacked on the door. That was all. 'Nothing to call out the guard for or to write home about.' "

"So Mars saved you from being rushed while you were busy with Roan," commented Bladen, "and then he was lucky enough to upset you just as a load of shot went past where your head ought to have been. Yet half an hour later you were trying to give him away! Talk about gratitude!"

Bruce said nothing. Stooping over the collie that lay drowsily at his feet, he rumpled the dog's classic head roughly. In the caress there was a world of unspoken remorse.

Yet he made no effort to set himself right in Horace's eyes. He could not explain to this friend of his that something had come crashing into his soul which made any sacrifice seem worth while.

"By the way," said Bladen, shifting the subject, "Miss Gates will be as safe up there, with Mars, as she'd be with a brace of automatic pistols. That Jackson White crowd has always looked on him with a sort of awe; ever since a bunch of them, down by the river, saw him round up those runaway sheep of yours that had taken to the water. It must have looked like a miracle to them, to see a dog use that amount of brainwork and training. They don't know any dogs but their own rabble of black wolf-mongrels and such hunting-dogs as happen to come through the mountains during the shooting season. To see a trained collie at work among a huddle of panic-crazed sheep was a revelation to

them. Miss Gates told me Manthy Shively asked her once
if Mars was 'really a devil or just a feller dressed up like a
dog.' "

"They'll have still more reason to be leery of him after
this," said Bruce, still stroking the dog's silken head. "He
half killed one of their black curs and he stood off another
of them, and he never got a single scratch. Besides that, he
dodged a smash from a stick Monk Shively tried to use on
him and he bit Monk's forearm to the bone. Yes, she'll be
safe, with Mars to look after her. Just the same, I've a
rotten feeling that we're not through with that crowd yet.
If it had been Tully Bemis to-day, instead of just the Shively
crew, I might not have gotten off so easily. Yes, and those
three black dogs of Tully's would have been a big order for
Mars to handle. Tully and his dogs are kings up there,
where might makes right."

"Bemis's two years in prison and the two other years that
he had to stay out of the way in Paterson, on account of
that Mitchell stabbing you told me about, must have given
him an invaluable education for handling his fellow-mountaineers," conjectured Bladen. "That and his tremendous
strength and his wild-beast pluck. It's a bad combination."

"And yet, with it all, the fool wastes his time prowling
around gullies and crannies, looking for treasure that probably never existed," laughed Bruce. "His time in prison
and in the Paterson slums didn't seem to teach him as much
as you think."

"You say the treasure 'probably never existed,' " argued
Horace. "How about the letter you read us the other day?
The one from your more or less worthy great-grandfather.
That seems to establish pretty clearly that the three Hes-

sians got to this region with the pay-chest and with Major Hough's casket, doesn't it? And it dovetails in pretty closely with the rumor among the Jackson Whites that there is treasure hidden somewhere up there."

Hardin shrugged his shoulders.

"Yes," he admitted. "I suppose I was wrong when I said it never existed. It may have existed, but that's no sign it exists now. Groot and Mann and Devries may have dug it up and gone somewhere with it, or they may have used it, bit by bit, to buy booze and tobacco and clothes. There's no reason to think it's still there. In fact, the idea is silly. Nearly all treasure yarns are."

"I don't like to think there's anything effeminate about me," said Bladen, half ashamed. "Yet by some rare freak, sometimes, I seem to have feminine intuitions. And usually they're right. Ever since you read us that letter I've had a hunch the treasure is there. I haven't been able to get it out of my mind. One of these days I'm going over to Auntie Groot's cabin again, at the edge of the Blue-eyed Nigger colony—if I can find my way back there—and I'm going to question her about it."

"What has she got to do with it?" asked Bruce. "Even if she is really the granddaughter of the Hessian who deserted, she isn't likely to know any more than the rest of the Jackson Whites. If she did, Tully Bemis would have tortured the secret out of her long before now."

"If he knew she had any idea of it, he would," agreed Bladen. "Just as he put that old recluse's feet in the fire, up near Suffern, to make him tell where his imaginary fortune was hidden. Eth Wallace told me about it. (Tully ought to have gotten a life sentence for that, instead of only

[59]

two years.) But he may not know she knows, or she may have made him believe she doesn't know, or he may be afraid of her. She's supposed to be a witch, isn't she?"

"She's the connecting link between the Blue-eyed Niggers and the Jackson Whites, anyhow," said Bruce, "witch or not. And both clans have a sort of scared veneration for her. The first time I ever set eyes on Tully Bemis he was sitting in the doorway of Auntie Groot's hut, gorging Indian corn cake and molasses that she had given him. I was a kid at the time. So was he. I was hunting up there, with my first gun, one my dad had given me for Christmas. I went past her shack. Most of us youngsters were afraid to go near it. So were the Jackson White brats. But with a real gun over my shoulder I felt as brave as a lion that day. So I kept on, close to her door. And there sat Tully Bemis, with no gun at all, being fed by her. It made me feel a sort of hero worship for him. I don't know whether or not he still keeps up the acquaintance and I don't know how she came to make a pet of him. He must have been a rather rough pet, even then."

"I'm going there some day," repeated Horace. "If it's true that she is well over a hundred years old, she might easily remember her grandfather, the original Groot, if he lived to any great age. I'm going to try to get her to talking about him——"

"And get chased with another kettle of hot water, for your pains?" supplemented Bruce. "Take my tip and keep away from there. If she has been able to keep the secret from Tully Bemis, she'll keep it from you. That is, if there is any secret; which there isn't. It's all rot. Just forget it. The only intuition I ever take any stock in is the intuition that's coming over me right now—an intuition that supper is ready for us and that I'm more than ready for supper. Come along and let's eat."

He started indoors. Mars got up to follow. Bruce motioned him back.

"What's the matter?" asked Bladen. "Old Mars isn't in disgrace, is he? Aren't you going to let him come into the dining-room, as he always does?"

"No," said Bruce, a crease of worry coming into his forehead. "No, I'm not. I want him to stay out here on guard. Now and all night. Nothing can ever set foot on this farm without Mars knowing it. There's a bare chance he may be needed to-night. By to-morrow the Shively crowd will have found some one to read my warning to them. But they may not be able to, till then. It's best to keep on the safe side. Fire is the one thing I dread; out here in the hinterland. Every farmer does."

"What has fire got to do with—?"

"Out of the jumble of howled and screeched language they pelted me with this afternoon, while I was lambasting Roan Shively," responded Hardin, "I caught a sentence from one of his sweet brothers. Monk, I think it was. It ran something like, '*Happen the red fox may run over your roof, for this*'!"

"The red fox?" queried Bladen, puzzled.

"It's an old English phrase," explained Bruce. "Like a lot of other old English phrases and words, it has been transplanted bodily into the vocabulary of the Jackson Whites. It is their allegorical way of threatening to set fire to my house and barns. It may have been just bluster. But I'm not taking chances."

[61]

"H'm!" mused Bladen. "But suppose Miss Gates had accepted your present and taken Mars home with her. Didn't think of that, did you?"

"Yes," said Bruce, curtly, "I did. I figured, in that case, you and I would have to mount guard, in turns, all night."

"She has done me a good turn, then," commented Horace, "to make up for the one I did her. She's given me a full night's sleep. I am gladder than ever that she didn't accept Mars. I'd have hated to sit up all night, just on the bare chance of seeing a 'red fox run over your roof.' "

"You'd have hated worse," said Hardin, grimly, "not to wake till after the roof had begun to cave in. Come along to supper. On watch, Mars, old boy!"

The night passed, and day crawled up over the eastward hills, with no menace to the Hardin farm. Presumably Bruce's missive had been read, or else the Shivelys conjectured he would be on watch.

Bruce Hardin was up with the sunrise. He had slept heavily and with no shadow of apprehension. Mars was on guard. After nightfall, no lightest step could sound, a furlong from the house, without the collie's hearing it from his mat on the porch and trotting forth to investigate.

Hardin knew the most stealthy incendiary could not creep up to the farthermost farm buildings without scent or sound of him reaching the watch-dog. Wherefore he himself had slept the sleep of healthy physical fatigue; albeit with a shotgun propped against the wall alongside his room door, in case Mars should sound a night alarm.

He awoke at sunrise. Long before Sibyl was ready to start on her morning journey to school Bruce was through with breakfast and with his first morning chores and was on the lookout for her.

"I wish she wasn't going till an hour or so later," said Bladen, wistfully. "By that time I'd have finished my morning stunt in the stable and be able to go up there with her. I'm going to follow up that antimony lead I told you about, unless you'd like me to help you with the corn."

"Chase ahead," answered Bruce. "A whole day of backbreak in a red-hot cornfield would undo all the good you've gained. It's enough for you to do the stable chores and the night milking, till you get some more flesh on your slat ribs."

Freely as he gave his consent, yet Hardin was ashamed of himself for being glad that Horace was to go up into the mountains an hour later than Sibyl and not as her escort.

Catching sight of the teacher coming out of the Wallace house with her bag of books, Bruce whistled to Mars and hurried across to intercept her. At sight of her Mars bounded forward in eager welcome. She stooped and patted him, then advanced to meet Bruce.

"I'm so glad you didn't change your mind about my taking him along," she said. "I've been looking forward to it all morning. He'll be glorious company for me. Won't you, Mars? And now we'll have to hurry. I'm late as it is."

"Mars," Hardin bade the collie, speaking slowly and with much distinctness as he indicated the girl, "*go* with her. *Stay* with her till she brings you home. *Stay*."

The dog understood. With marked diminution of his gay demeanor he turned his back on his master and fell soberly into step beside Sibyl.

Off started the two, Bruce Hardin watching them out of sight before he went back to his own day's work.

Sibyl walked fast. She was not as late as she had implied

[63]

to Bruce. But she was minded to take the southern and
longer path to the schoolhouse, in order not to pass the
Shively cabin. She dreaded revisiting the scene of yesterday's encounter, despite her brave words to Hardin and
the others.

Up the southerly trail she hurried, Mars close beside her
and once in a while leading the way when the path was too
narrow for them to walk abreast. Presently the dog checked
his advance and stood looking questioningly up the twisting
way. A man was descending toward them.

CHAPTER

5

AT the next turn they came face to face with him. He was gigantic and shaggy, and in the late twenties; roughly clad, but less disreputable in dress and in poise than the bulk of the Jackson Whites. A pick-ax was over his shoulder.

Sibyl had seen Tully Bemis several times before, but never at such close quarters. In view of her treatment from the Shivelys, she was aware of a flutter of nervousness. Mars, too, growled and stiffened to fierce attention. But whether he resented the oncoming of Bemis or of the three lean black mongrels that slouched at Bemis's heels, Sibyl could not guess.

Sibyl caught the collie detainingly by the ruff. Tully spoke a gruff word to the three mongrels which had started savagely forward. Instantly they came to heel. If the brutes did not love their giant master, at least they feared him enough to obey implicitly. They crowded behind him as he stood to one side to allow the girl to pass.

This action of his was of Chesterfieldian courtesy, judged from mountaineer standards. Sibyl wondered at it. She wondered still more at the grin of genuine amusement that brightened his heavy face.

"Morning, Teacher!" he hailed her as she passed on her way, the collie still held by the ruff. "My name's Bemis— Tully Bemis. I know you by sight, but I s'pose you don't know me. My kid nephew, Cleppy, is jawing about you all the time. You're li'ble to put some sense in his head, the way you're teaching him. He's improved a heap."

Sibyl stopped in her upward climb and gazed at him in wide-eyed amaze. This was the first hint of praise or even of good will she had received from any grown Jackson White in all her eight months of work in the mountains. She wondered if she had heard the giant aright.

"Thank you," she said, pleasantly. "Cleppy is my star pupil. I have great hopes for him. I'm glad you think he is improving."

"He sure is," declared Tully, adding, conscientiously: "He used to be such a numbwit that there wasn't but one direction his brains could go. They was bound to improve, if they moved at all. Not that that takes away none from your credit in learning him like you have. His pa wanted him to quit schooling after he'd learned the A B C and a wee peckle about ciphering. But I made him let the kid keep on. I been wanting to see you and tell you I like how you're doing up yonder. I'm a scholard, myself. I was to Oakland school three terms when I was no bigger'n Cleppy.

I got learned a lot in reform school, too. There's few enough up here can read and write. One of 'em brang me some reading to do, only last night. Likewise I done it."

His face expanded into a grin once more, at the recollection.

"Yep," he went on, in response to the girl's polite look of inquiry. "A woman brang me a writing to read. A real funny writing it was, too. Maybe you'd be int'rested to read it, ma'am? It's kind of wrote about you. Or maybe it ain't. You'd best take a squint at it and see what you think."

He dug deep in a side pocket of his greasy khaki trousers and pulled forth, along with his pipe and tobacco pouch, a wad of paper.

This he spread out clumsily and handed to Sibyl. It was dirty and repulsive of aspect. Yet the girl, civilly, forced herself to take it. As she began to read the blurredly thumbed characters, her face changed color. Glancing up, she noted that Bemis's black eyes were observing her expression with eager intentness.

By mighty effort she made her face a mask and read on.

"Well, ma'am?" demanded Bemis, in quite a different voice, as she finished. "What you gotta say to that? Does it int'rest you or don't it?"

Vexed and troubled by the mountaineer's look, Sibyl dropped her eyes to the soiled scrap of paper and read it once more. It was an envelope back on which was printed in pencil Bruce's message to the Shivelys:

I shall telephone the sheriff of Bergen County to-night. If I am ever found dead or if my house or ricks are burned, he will bring a posse up here and land you all in jail for life.

BRUCE HARDIN.

And Hardin had told her merely that he had had a "fatherly" chat with the Shivelys, who henceforth would not molest her! This fierce message did not seem in any way fatherly. Why should he write as though he were in danger of death from the Shivelys? What had led up to this printed warning?

Again Sibyl recalled the splash of blood on Mars's frill and the abrasions on Hardin's palms. Something had happened, something ferocious and deadly, up there at the Shively cabin—something which made it safe for her to go alone through the mountains, but which menaced Bruce's life.

The thrill that had surged over her, at Hardin's reticence concerning his adventure, swept across her heart afresh. There was more than mere womanly curiosity in her yearning to piece together the happenings which had led up to this message's writing.

Meanwhile, Tully Bemis was watching her intently from under his shaggy black brows, his dark eyes shining snakelike in their effort to read her thoughts.

"Well," he repeated, "does it int'rest you, ma'am, or don't it?"

Sibyl's soft lips closed on an admission that she knew nothing about the matter. In the first place, Bemis would not believe her. It was not in mountaineer comprehension that any man could have done something as dashing as Bruce had done and not brag windily to his womenfolk about it. Moreover, it was only by letting Tully think she knew the story that she could hope to get him to tell her more of it.

"Yes," she said, quietly, "it interests me. Thank you for showing me the message."

As she spoke she slipped the greasy envelope into her school bag.

"It has served its turn," she said in response to Bemis's gesture as he reached out for it. "I am going to keep it as a souvenir."

If she expected opposition, she received none. Bemis nodded approval; grinning again.

"You got good nerve," he told her, patronizingly. "Not that you wouldn't have—the way valley men treat their women. Women down yonder don't have nothing to be scairt of. If they lived up here they'd soon be learnt better. That was why you didn't get scairter when Roan was going to slam you with his belt—the swill-brained old fool!"

He spoke in high contempt of his fellow-mountaineer. Not expecting to hear even this oblique form of denunciation from a Jackson White, against woman-beating, the girl stared at him in new astonishment. Again he answered her look, expatiating on the theme.

"When his wife come to me last night to git me to read that writing," said he, "she told me about how Shively pretty near got shot by that spindly Bladen cuss and then how Hardin whaled the skin off'n Roan's back. I told her Roan got off damn easy. If Bladen hadn't happened along, I told her, you'd have been belted and maybe injured serious by it. But whether you was injured serious or not, you'd 'a' gone back to the valley, and told. And I know them valley folks well enough to know Shively would be in Hackensack jail by now; and maybe a bunch of farmers would be up here, burning our housen and acting up scand'lous, to get even for one of their women being whipped. I know those folks down there. Roan acted like a plumb idjit. I told her so."

"Thank you," said the girl, doubtfully.

"Yep," continued Bemis, "I told her it would 'a' been a heap sensibler to come up behind you, unbeknownst, when you was walking along that path at the top of the rock, and give you an ac'dental shove down it. He could duck outa sight, and you'd have a broke arm or leg or head; that'd hurt you worse'n a belting. And nobody'd get in trouble over it. But Roan always was a simple."

The man was ingenuously in earnest. Listening, Sibyl was reminded of a sentence in an essay she had read lately on Richard III. The sentence ran, "He did not have bad morals; he had no morals at all."

"Well," resumed Bemis, "Roan sure paid good for what he laid out to do. He's in bed. They's a-gabbing about it all through the mountains by this time. From Ringwood to Pompton. He's due to git hisself laughed at, plenty. It was a good stunt of Hardin's, too. There ain't a mountaineer from here to York State line, after this, that'll dare lay the tip of his finger on you, ma'am. Not a one, barring me, and I got no reason to. Well, I'm a-keeping you from gitting to school. So long, ma'am," he finished, sociably, snapping his fingers to his three black dogs to precede him down the trail toward the valley.

The mongrels obeyed his gesture. As they passed close to Mars, one of them snapped furtively at the collie's hip. Mars snarled in angry resentment and tugged fiercely to break free from Sibyl's restraining grasp and assail the black dog.

Tully Bemis lavished a heartfelt kick on the transgressing mongrel which sent the poor brute and his two fellows scuttling down the path in terror.

"That big collie of Hardin's is jest sp'iling for a fight, ain't he?" commented Bemis. "We don't see him up in these parts very often. How's he happen to be six inches away from Hardin's heels to-day? He never was before."

"Mr. Hardin lent him to me—" began Sibyl; but Bemis broke in with a wide grin of comprehension.

"To sic him onto anyb'dy that pesters you!" he cried, enlightened. "Grand idee! Only there was no need. Roan's belt done the work, so far's you're c'ncerned. Nob'dy's going to pester you none, and Hardin's losing his wuthless dog's comp'ny for the day, all for nothing. Well, I must be getting to my potato-digging," he ended, shouldering his pick and starting to follow his curs down toward the lower levels of the mountain.

His scoffing tone toward Hardin and Mars had an unaccountably irritating effect on Sibyl. Her wontedly placid temper stirred. Speaking with seeming innocence, she called after the departing man:

"I didn't know people used pick-axes for digging potatoes. Are you sure you're not going treasure-hunting, instead?"

Before the ill-advised words were fairly spoken the girl regretted them. She bit her lip in self-vexation at her indiscreet question.

The effect on Tully Bemis was electrical. The mockingly

civil manner he had maintained toward her fell from him like a garment. Dropping the pick, he was at her side in a single bound. His face was distorted and black.

"What'nhell are you gassing about?" he challenged, hotly.

His ferocious manner changed the girl's brief regret into honest indignation. She tightened her grip on Mars's ruff as the collie growled up at the menacing giant. Much she longed to set the dog free and bid him follow his own will. Too wise to do this, nevertheless she was urged by her temper to make up for the physical restraint by tormenting still further the scowling mountaineer.

"What's that jabber about treasure?" stormed Bemis, stung at her fleck on the raw of his monomania. "What treasure are you blatting about? Hey? *I* don't know about no treasure."

"No?" she queried, in the same provoking mock innocence, resolved not to let him see he had angered her, yet in no wise minded to let him off scot-free. "I thought perhaps you might have heard of it. It was buried in these Ramapo Mountains by three Hessian deserters. One of them was the grandfather of a woman known as Auntie Groot. Did you never hear about it? I'm told there is one man up here who spends most of his time looking for it. I hear others are interested in it, too."

She turned, to continue her belated climb toward the schoolhouse. But, on the instant, Tully Bemis was barring her path. As she still sought to pass by him, he thrust out a hand to detain her. Snarling, Mars slashed at the dirty hand. Tully snatched it back, with incredible speed; but held his ground.

[72]

"*Who* else is a-looking for it?" he cried, his big voice thick and shaking. "Who is—?"

"Why shouldn't anybody or everybody?" she countered, coolly enough. "It belongs to nobody now. It belongs to anyone who can find it. Why shouldn't people look for it— any of them who care to? Surely you didn't suppose you were the only man who knew about it?"

From his dark-flushed face and amazement it was very evident that he had supposed himself to be the only active searcher for the hoard, and that the fact of valley men knowing about it and seeking it was a blow between the eyes to him.

"Who else is a-looking for it?" he repeated, deep down in his throat.

"Who isn't?" she retorted, morbidly glad to sting the bully who was trying to intimidate her.

In the bottom of her heart she realized she was not only doing a risky thing, but one unworthy of her own dignity, in thus tormenting the mountaineer. But her nerves were still ajump from her experience of the day before. Also, any attempt at bullying or brow-beating always served to rouse her to retaliation.

The giant glowered murderously down into her unruffled face and level eyes. Then, shifting his method of attack, he asked, suddenly:

"Where did *you* hear about it? Who told you?"

She recognized the question as a new mode of seeking to find out who besides himself was hunting for the treasure. But, her first short gust of indignation gone, she was wearying of the sorry sport of bully-baiting. She put an end to the absurd scene by saying:

[73]

"Mr. Hardin read us all about it in a letter he found in the attic of his house. A letter from his great-grandfather. It told all about the stealing and hiding of a British pay-chest, and the jewel-casket. That is all I know about the matter and that is all I care to know about it."

As she finished speaking she stepped forward. To her surprise, Tully Bemis made no effort to stop her. He stepped, or rather stumbled, aside, and let her pass. The dark red had ebbed suddenly from his unshaven face, leaving it sallow and drawn. He was looking at her blankly, as might a sleep-walker; though far to the back of his staring eyes a queer light was beginning to smolder.

On she went, with Mars beside her. As she reached the next twist of path she glanced back. Tully Bemis still stood there, swaying a little, his lips moving. Then, as she moved on, she saw him start blunderingly down the trail, leaving the pick-ax where it lay.

Sibyl was thoroughly disgusted with herself. Reviewing her interview with Bemis, she could not now see how she had brought herself down toward the man's level in such fashion as to seek to annoy him. The fact that he had spoken mockingly to her, and then had assumed an air of threat, did not justify her in her own eyes for deigning to speak to him as she had done.

It was not like her, at all. She found herself going contemptuously over the memory of her own words as over those of some stranger. She hoped Bruce might never hear of it nor know she had stepped so far off the pedestal whereon he seemed to have placed her.

As to any possible complications arising from what she had said, that thought did not occur to her for an instant.

She was too busy upbraiding herself for her loss of dignity.

Bruce Hardin came home from the fields at noontime, hot and hungry. He stopped on the kitchen stoop to scrape the mud and loam off his boot soles and to wash in the tin basin set there for the purpose.

As he was splashing the cold water over his hot face, old Mrs. Wilk, who cooked and kept house for Bladen and himself, came to the kitchen door and peered out at him in surprise.

"That's funny!" said she.

"What is?" asked Bruce, rubbing his face dry with the towel from the nail above the basin. "What's 'funny'?"

"Why, it's funny how you could have come downstairs and through my kitchen and out here, without me seeing you," explained Mrs. Wilk. "I was putting my set of bread into the oven. But I didn't have my back turned more than a few seconds. And I didn't hear you at all. I was waiting for you, too, to ask you to step on the newspapers I laid down there, after I scrubbed my kitchen floor this morning. You must have walked on your tiptoes."

"Mrs. Wilk," said Hardin, solemnly, as he tossed aside the crumpled towel, "it's a deep and dark mystery. I had been hoping to guard it forever. But now I'll divulge it. The reason you didn't hear me come through the kitchen is that I haven't been in the kitchen to-day. That is the only reason you didn't hear me. Don't tell anybody. It's a secret."

As a rule, his good-natured bantering was a joy to the lonely old housekeeper. But this time she did not greet his feeble flippancy with so much as a smile. Instead, she looked at him in growing surprise.

"Then," she demanded, "if you didn't come through the kitchen, how did you get out here?"

"I came up from the south meadow," he said, "and straight across to the stoop, from the barn. Why?"

"But you *couldn't!*" she insisted. "You went up to your room first, and then up-attic and then back to your room again. I heard you rummaging around in there, no end, most likely leaving a passel of things for me to pick up and put in order, as usual, I suppose. I—"

"Hold on! I haven't—"

"But how you got downstairs without me so much as hearing you and then across the kitchen, with me in it, and out here onto the stoop—without me seeing you—"

"I tell you I didn't," laughed Bruce, amused at her garrulous perplexity. "I haven't been indoors since I started to work this morning. If you heard anyone upstairs in my room just now, it must have been Mr. Bladen. Probably he is looking for a pair of my hiking boots. His own are always wearing out. Only last week he came and asked me if he might please borrow them. I told him he could and I asked why he had gone through the formality of asking my leave. He said, 'Because I can't find them.' That's what he must be looking for up there now."

"Not him," denied Mrs. Wilk. "In the first place, skinny as he is, he walks as heavy as a team of mules. Those fine roomy feet of his would be grand for stamping out forest fires. No. This man moved as light as a cat. Lighter than you do; light as you are on your feet. I wondered why you was so quiet up there. If it hadn't been that a mouse can be heard all over this old house, I'd never have heard you at all. In the second place, Mr. Bladen started off for the

[76]

mountains two hours ago, with his satchel and that funny little hammer of his. He stopped in the kitchen and got me to give him a couple of sandwiches for his lunch. Then I saw him start off across the fields for the bridge. If he'd come back, I'd have heard him. Every step he takes always sounds like three men moving a piano. Nope, it wasn't Mr. Bladen. And since you choose to make believe it wasn't you——"

She checked herself. Directly above their heads a window screen thumped softly, as though some one had raised it, to climb out of the rear window of Hardin's room on to the kitchen roof, and as if it had slipped from his grasp.

CHAPTER

6

BRUCE hurried through the kitchen and up the back stairs, to investigate. The door of his room was shut. He turned the knob. The door was locked—a thing that did not happen once a year.

Bruce wasted no time. Some one was in that room; as had been proven by the slipping of the window screen. A locked door stood between the intruder and the room's rightful occupant.

Stepping back, Hardin braced his heel against the opposite wall of the narrow passage; then flung himself, thus reinforced, against the locked door. With all his weight and with all his muscular strength he hurled his shoulder at the door, just above the lock.

There was a splintering sound as the tough old oak cracked under the mighty impact. The ancient lock snapped like rotten pine. The door flew open, inward.

Into the room catapulted Hardin. As he did so, something smote him crashingly on the top of the head. The air was full of multicolored rockets and pinwheels, through which he plunged a million miles downward into black oblivion.

Mrs. Wilk, waiting curiously at the foot of the stairs, heard him burst open the door, then thud heavily to the carpet. She called, quaveringly, up to him. He made no reply.

Now none of this made an atom of sense to the housekeeper. Accustomed to men's impatient ways, she could well imagine his breaking the lock sooner than come downstairs and search for the key wherewith he had supposedly locked the door when he went out that morning. Nor did she blame him for locking his room when Bladen was so prone to borrow his belongings.

But the sound of his fall and his non-reply to her query —these might be more serious. Perhaps in hurling himself into the room in that crazy fashion he might have struck his head against a table or against a bedpost and been knocked senseless. It would be well to find out.

Her narrow-caliber brain too busily taken up with this hypothesis to recall the earlier sound of the window screen or to conjecture what it might mean, Mrs. Wilk trotted up the steep old stairs to the rescue.

The door was wide open. Indeed, it was swung far back toward the wall. In the middle of the room lay Bruce Hardin. Prone on his face he lay sprawled, arms and legs wide. A trickle of blood oozed from his cut scalp, down the side of his cheek, and on to the old-fashioned Brussels carpet that covered the floor.

Beside his head lay one of the heavy brass candlesticks that stood usually on the room's antique Hepplewhite dresser. The candlestick was bent almost double from the force of the blow that had been struck with it.

The housekeeper cried out, in cackling horror. She ran forward and knelt rheumatically down beside the unconscious man, lifting his bleeding head and trying to find the extent of his injuries.

The room door, behind her, creaked ever so slightly, as though it were swinging part way shut. But for the moment Mrs. Wilk had no ears for it and no thought for anything but the smitten Bruce.

"Vinegar and brown paper will be best till I can phone the doctor," she mused, half aloud, as she fingered the scalp wound. "How'd he ever manage to do it, I wonder? Men are so clumsy—always falling over theirselves!"

Then her eyes fell on the bent candlestick. For the first time she gave conscious heed to it and wondered what it might be doing there.

"Got jarred off'n the dresser, most likely, when he hit the floor with such a thump," she told herself; adding at once, "No, it didn't, neither! It couldn't have hopped ten feet, like it must of, if that's how it happened to fall. And what on earth did the poor boy hit his head against? There ain't a piece of furniture, anywheres, near enough. He——"

Slowly her mind began to connect Hardin's fall with the bent candlestick. Still more slowly, she turned her head toward the door, her memory at last registering the faint creaking sound she had heard a minute earlier.

When she had come into the room the door had been

swung far back. She remembered that. Even in the shock of the moment her housekeeperly soul had wondered if the knob had gouged into the plaster.

But now the door was more than half shut.

Whoever had hidden behind it must have made a safe escape while she was working over his victim. Then, her memory working in reverse order, as so often in times of sudden stress, Mrs. Wilk recalled the sound she and Bruce had heard in this room.

The slipping window screen—the bent candlestick—the stricken Hardin—the half closing of the door! She put them in their rightful order, at last.

Having done so, Mrs. Wilk sat down hard and began to screech right industriously for help.

After a few moments of this lung-expanding exercise she realized that there was nobody within call. Summoning all her courage, she got up and made her way to the hall telephone, below.

First of all, she summoned Bruce's next-door neighbor, Ethan Wallace, who was just finishing a hasty noonday dinner, preparatory to getting back to his spring work.

Then, in succession, she called up four doctors—all of whom were out. For this is the way, in the average rural neighborhood. A doctor, who is worth sending for, is sent for so often that he is far more likely to be out than in when he is wanted in a hurry. A doctor who is usually at home is prone to be one not worth summoning. Moreover, the average rural doctor has strong sportsmanly tendencies. In early May, in northern New Jersey, the trout season is at its height. Mighty is the lure of rod and fly to an overworked country physician.

Mrs. Wilk had just called the fourth of the absent doctors

when Ethan Wallace came bustling in, his hired man with him.

Before asking questions, the two men lifted Bruce to his bed and began to bathe his cut scalp. Wallace, with skillful fingers, fingered the hurt.

"Don't feel like a fracture to me," he remarked, cheerfully. "Besides, it's on the top of the head, kind of toward the front. That's where the bone is thickest. But it's a thundering big wallop he got, at that. Ken, you hustle over home and get the car. Drive down to Post's Brook and take a squint along the banks for a half mile or so each way. I guess you'll run across Doc Spurling somewheres there. I saw him driving past this morning, with that old yeller suit of his on, the one he goes fishing in. Bring him up here in a rush.

"Mrs. Wilk, have you got some old linen, soft enough to make a bandage of? Maybe Bruce has some old handkerchiefs that'd do. You might look in his bureau. Top drawer, most likely. Oh," he continued, glancing over at the dresser, "you've been looking in there already, hey? The top drawer is wide open, and all the other drawers, too, and most of the stuff in them dumped out on to the floor. You must have been dretful confused."

"I haven't touched any of them," shrilled the old woman. "That was done by the murderer who hit him with the candlestick."

"What murderer are you talking about?" demanded Wallace, who had been able to gather nothing from her incoherent telephone talk except that Hardin was badly hurt.

Now, her words and sentences tumbling over one another, with irritating little eddies formed of many repetitions of the less important details, Mrs. Wilk spattered the whole story at Wallace.

As she talked, the dumfounded man's eyes roamed the room. Everywhere drawers were pulled out and their contents manhandled. The desk in one corner had been broken literally to pieces, as if in quest of a secret drawer. The pillows had been slit open, as had the mattress. The room bore myriad signs of an awkward but swiftly efficient search. One pillow-case was missing. Apparently it had been pressed into service as a bag for carrying off the loot.

Bruce Hardin twisted convulsively and groaned. Then his eyes opened in a drunken way and he stared about him.

The blow that had knocked him out had caused but the mildest concussion of the brain. Wallace had been right in his guess that there was no fracture. As a football warrior recovers from a knockout occasioned by a cleated boot's contact with his jaw in a scrimmage, as a knocked-out pugilist recovers from the blow that wins the bout, so Hardin came to himself.

His great muscular strength and perfect condition and his youth were potent factors. The cap he had worn, as well as his shock of somewhat long hair, had broken the full force of the blow. Moreover, an antique brass candlestick, be it ever so massive, has not the resistance quality of a bar of iron. The bending of the candlestick had lessened the power of the concussion.

"Don't try to talk!" commanded Wallace as Bruce mumbled something unintelligible by way of query. "And don't you go plaguing him with questions, neither, Mrs. Wilk. Leave him lay as he is till Doc gets here. I'm going up attic to see if you was right when you said you heard noises there."

Five minutes later Wallace was back in the bedroom. Bruce was lying with half-shut eyes, a crease of pain between his brows. Mrs. Wilk was swabbing his head with stinging vinegar.

"Attic looks like a hurrah's nest," reported Wallace, speaking low to the housekeeper. "Every trunk is bust wide open. That little old haircloth trunk is clean empty. The one Bruce's gre'granther's letters was in. Beats the Dutch, don't it? Lots of good stuff laying around the floor, up attic, where it had been slung out'n the trunks. Some of it worth any thief's bother, to steal. Not a bit of it touched. And see those things here, dumped out'n the drawers. Not a one gone. Not even that sort of flat pin-cushion with Bruce's scarf-pins quilted into it. Not even the silver frame on that desk picture of his mother's. It don't make sense. I wonder how—"

The advent of Doctor Spurling put a stop to his conjectures. Clad in faded yellow khaki and smelling of fish scales and rank tobacco, the physician came busily into the room and crossed to the bed.

"I sent your hired man over to my house for my medicine case, Wallace," said he, bending over the patient. "But I doubt if I'll need it. This boy begins to look as good as new, again. If you hadn't sent for me in such a rush, there'd have been grave danger of his getting well before I could reach him. Now then, Hardin, let's examine that bump. Lord! Who has been trying to make pickles out of your hair, with vinegar? You smell like a cider mill. H'm!

[84]

Hurts when I do that, hey? Set your teeth, because I'm going to play tunes on that scalp of yours. . . . Just as I thought. Not a sign of any fracture. You're in luck. By to-morrow you'll be as well as ever you were—till you try to clap a hat on that sore dome. Lie still while I dress it. Don't try to talk. There's nothing the matter with you but what the police reports call 'abrasions and contusions.' How'd it happen, Wallace? Did he fall off a haystack? Lucky he landed on the toughest part of him."

When Horace Bladen came home from the day's geological wanderings he found Bruce sitting on the back porch, a loose cap pulled low down on his brow, to hide a neat white bandage.

"Just a crack on the head," reported Hardin, in reply to his chum's astonished inquiry. "Nothing to get excited about. It has left me with a splitting headache that is beginning at last to stop splitting. It's left me with a sore scalp that doesn't hurt any more, unless I touch it. That's all. All except the queer mystery of it."

In as few words as possible he told what had happened. As he finished his narrative he saw Sibyl Gates cross the bridge, with Mars galloping ahead of her. She was on her way home after an uneventful day of teaching. Bruce got halfway to his feet to go forward and meet her. Then he checked himself.

"I don't want her to see me with this thing on my head," he told Bladen. "She'd ask about it, and I'd have to lie. I made Ethan promise not to tell her. You know how frightened women are whenever there's a burglar scare in the neighborhood. She'd lie awake all night for a week, thinking she heard robbers. I've warned Wallace, and Mrs. Wilk, too, not to blab."

Putting his fingers to his lips, he whistled shrilly and long. At the summons Mars left the girl and came rushing across the fields toward his master, like a red-gold meteor, his shining coat beautiful against the early green of the grass.

"It would have been more civil in me to go and meet her and bring Mars home myself," said Hardin. "I'll get you to take him over to her when she starts in the morning; but by that time perhaps I can take off this silly bandage, so she won't notice I've been hit."

Mars cleared the veranda steps at one leap, and came frisking up to his master in wild eagerness of welcome after the long day's absence. Bruce patted the dog, and spoke to him as to a fellow-human. When at last the collie had curled up at his feet, Hardin went on:

"There's a genuine mystery about this thing, Horace. In the first place, some thief got into the house while I was away and while you were away and while Mars was away. Nobody could have gotten inside the dooryard, with Mars on guard. This had to happen on the first day in his life when the good old dog was off the job. Funny coincidence, isn't it? Of course, while Mrs. Wilk was pottering around the kitchen alone, any light-footed and light-fingered crook could have gotten into the house from the far side.

"Probably he didn't know I come home to lunch every day when I'm near enough. So he overstayed his time. Then when he heard me on the stoop he tried to get out of the window of my room. He had locked the door. I suppose he did it in case Mrs. Wilk should happen to go there. I broke in, and he swatted me, from behind, with the first thing he could pick up. He put me out. Then he hid behind the bedroom door till Mrs. Wilk came in. As soon as she was busy over me he sneaked out and made a clean get-away."

"But where does the mystery come in?" asked Bladen. "Thus far, it's just an ordinary piece of robbery and assault."

"Do you know what he stole?"

"No," answered Bladen, "and I didn't like to ask, for fear you'd think I was worrying more over anything of mine he happened to take than over your accident. But—"

"He didn't take anything of yours," said Bruce, "except some scribbled notes you had left on your desk and some torn letters out of your waste-basket."

"What?" sputtered Horace, in wonder.

"But he took every letter and paper out of my room and out of the attic," went on Hardin. "Took them all. Cleaned them out and carried them off in a pillow-case. Not a single printed page, but every line of writing that he could lay hands on. He even went through the pockets of my clothes, hanging in the closets, and emptied them. He took every letter and everything else in writing. All old Colonel Hardin's letters, too. A clean sweep. And not one other thing did he touch. None of my jewelry or my watch or anything else. What do you make of that?"

Bladen stared blankly.

"I don't understand," he protested.

"Neither do I. There is where the mystery comes in.

Why should any sane man want to steal all the letters and other written papers in the house, and leave the really valuable things? And if a lunatic did it, how did he have brain enough to do it all so cunningly and to make his getaway as he did?"

"It doesn't make sense!" exclaimed Bladen. "Neither of us has any incriminating letters—anything that would be of use to a blackmailer. And if we had, why should he carry off the old deeds and the other written papers, as well as the letters? It's insane!"

"I've been pummeling my brains over it, all afternoon," said Hardin. "And I can't make head or tail of it. Suppose *you* take a turn at the puzzle for a while, now? Maybe you'll hit on the answer."

But, though the friends talked late into the evening, neither of them could hazard the remotest guess. A quarter mile distant, Sibyl Gates sat at work on her school routine for the next day. She alone could have put two and two together and have solved the mystery by dint of her talk with Tully Bemis that morning. But, thanks to Hardin's request to Wallace, the girl did not even know Bruce's house had been robbed.

Two miles away, as the crow flies, Tully Bemis sat doubled over a rickety deal table, by light of a sputtering kerosene lamp, in a cabin which came nearer looking like a decent abode than did any of its neighboring shacks.

On the table in front of him were piled high the motley aggregation of letters and other papers he had brought back from his daring midday raid on Bruce Hardin's home. Since early afternoon, he had sat thus, laboriously poring over the vast pile of written matter. Sunrise next morning found him still at work on it, with smarting eyes and dulled senses.

His fourteen hours of unaccustomed literary labor had brought him no results. Into his wily brain had flashed this audacious plan, the instant Sibyl had spoken to him so indiscreetly of Colonel Hardin's letter. To Bemis, naturally, this had meant that there was a full description of the treasure, in the letter or letters, and probably more or less full directions for finding it. The chance seemed to him well worth the risk. In order not to miss the right paper, he had stolen every scrap of writing in the house he could lay his hands on.

Among the rest was the old colonel's letter which Bruce had read aloud three days earlier. But even this gave the quest-crazed mountaineer no definite inspiration.

At sunrise he lurched to his feet.

"It's there, somewheres!" he muttered, half-aloud. "She said so. I missed it. But next time I won't miss it. There's better ways than the one I tried. . . . Better ways—for me. But maybe not for *him!*"

CHAPTER

7

TULLY BEMIS got up and stretched himself. His giant body was cramped from long hours of bending above the heap of papers. His eyes were throbbing. The flicker of the cheap old-fashioned kerosene lamp had strained cruelly his eye nerves and had given the man a headache.

The lamp had burned itself out, unnoted. The oil reek from its smoldering wick filled the unventilated cabin. Clumsily, stamping and kicking to restore circulation to his numb legs, Bemis lurched out into the open.

The shack he quitted was squalid enough, judged by civilized standards. Yet it was perhaps the most pretentious of any of the far-scattered Jackson White habitations. It was nearly a century old. It had been built before the era of cabins whose chief material consisted of stolen barn doors, slats from torn-down village houses, scrap tin, and similar cast-offs.

The Bemis house was of hewn logs, cunningly chinked with clay that had grown to mortar hardness. It had a large room on the ground floor and a small closet-like room off it on either side. A flight of real, if primitive, steps led to the unceiled loft.

There was a small and high window in every room, a touch of elegance made perfect by the fact that the windows were of good glass and frame and that one of them actually slid up and down—a triumph of luxury. Behind the house was a shed, better built than many a Jackson White family dwelling.

In the log cabin Tully had been born, as had his sire and granddam before him. Here he had lived alone—except for his sojourns in jail and in Paterson—since the death of his mother, twelve years earlier. From this ancestral castle he ruled as local overlord of the mountaineers, his incredible strength and his courage and superior education and brain making him easily the master of his slab-sided neighbors.

For a minute he stood on the door-stone, looking out across the billowing miles of springtime forest. The glory of the early woodland morning and the swelling chorus of bird songs and the ice-clear bracing air—all were lost on him. The mountaineer was used to these things. They did not stir or interest him.

Yet the freshness of the dawn wind began to disperse the mists from his brain. Deep inhalations of the chill mountain air drove from his lungs the oil reek and the sick closeness of the room he had quitted.

He stood there, pondering. Presently he turned back into

the house and gathered up the great riffle of paper, stuffing it into the air-tight stove and setting it alight. Up in one commingled blaze went old Colonel Hardin's quaint letters to his wife, along with many a sweeter memory of ancient days and with scores of later epistles, written deeds, and the like.

Bemis did not stay to watch the immolation of a hundred and fifty years of letters. As soon as he saw the paper well alight, he jammed his greasy hat on his uncombed shock of hair and set forth, across the ridge trails and through undergrowth tangles, in a straight line and with the deceptively mile-eating slouch of the true Jackson White. Unbidden, his three dogs fell into line behind him.

Past one or two clumps of hovels he made his way—tiny settlements which were scarce astir at such an hour. Lean black dogs lounged in the beaten-dirt dooryards. They got to their feet with cringing truculence as he came near. But at closer sight or scent of him and his ferocious curs, they shrank back and let him go his way in peace.

Here and there a tousled mountaineer, newly arisen, hailed him with grumpy or fawning deference. He paid no heed, but swung on. Toward the northwest he was headed. In that direction, for nearly two miles, he tramped, his three big black mongrels pattering along at his heels. Not once did the trio take courage to come abreast of him. Long since he had taught them to follow and not to risk a kick by pushing past him.

He left behind him the nearer settlements of his kind, and crossed a gully and mounted another ridge. This ridge marked the strictly kept boundary between the Jackson White territory and the smaller tract occupied by the Blue-eyed Niggers. At the further base of the ridge shimmered a little pond. Beyond it a clutter of huts strewed a valley cup set high in the hills.

Here dwelt a colony of the Blue-eyed Niggers. Here, and within a few miles of here, their ancestors had lived since the first group of runaway negro slaves from the Pompton region had fled hither to cast in their lot with the handful of degenerate Lenape Indians whose village bordered the handkerchief-sized spring pond.

To this cross-breed settlement had fared the three Hessian deserters during the American Revolution, to lord it over the black-and-tans and to change the physiognomy of the latters' descendants.

Over the pond slanted a sycamore tree. One side of the semi-horizontal trunk bulged slightly. The bulge was caused by the body of a youth who was stretched, panther-like and graceful, along the tree, dangling a cotton fish-line into the water.

The boy was slender and lithe. His clothes were raggedly rudimentary. His hair was wavy and blackish, with a tinge of red in it. His complexion was that of a mulatto, but with a hint of copper. His nose was straight and his lips were thin. His big eyes were light blue, standing forth startlingly from his dusky face.

This was one of the Blue-eyed Niggers—a lad scarce past his middle teens, yet already a husband and a father. His wife (who was also his aunt) being ill, he had been forced to do his own breakfast fishing this day.

He does not come into our story again, yet I have squandered a few words of description on him, as he was typical of a race—or rather, of a sub-race—that exists within thirty

miles of New York City, and yet which is as distinct from
any other as a Hottentot is distinct from a Greek. Isolation
and continual inbreeding has kept the type intact among
the few survivors of the Indian-Negro-German blend.

Without descending the ledge toward the settlement,
Tully Bemis kept along the ridge crest for another quarter
mile. Then he dipped down into a natural hollow on the
farther side and found himself in a tiny clearing in whose
center was a two-room log hovel somewhat smaller than
his own, but of greater age and built with even greater
stanchness. Except from part of the ridge, the hut and clearing were invisible amid the press of trees and bushes and
higher ground. An outsider might roam within a furlong
of it without suspecting its presence. For sheltered position
it was scarce surpassed by Tully's moonshine still, in a hidden gully, a mile to southward.

In the open doorway squatted a bent and withered
woman, incredibly old and shrunken. From her high-
cheekboned mummy face piercing black eyes blazed forth
with a spirit that age had not been able to conquer. Her
long-nailed hands were skinny brown claws. Yet, just now,
they were whipping the contents of a yellow bowl between
her knees with the vigor of a girl.

She was barefoot. Her wrapper of ragged calico once
had been fire red. Now all its color was bleached or stained
away, save for an occasional line of fading scarlet at some
split seam.

She did not look up, nor cease from beating the batter
in the yellow bowl, as Tully Bemis came in sight. But as he
stood looking down at her, before descending the steep
ridgeside to her cabin door, she said, as if to herself:

"Child, the cakes are ready to bake. Come eat. I heard you when you left your house."

Her English was good—when she did not drop into north Jersey Dutch for a word or sentence, as sometimes she did in excitement or anger. Her language was purer than that of her mountain neighbors, though the reedy old voice had an occasional guttural note in it that might have been a throw-back to either her Hessian or her Lenape ancestry.

Well versed in her ways, Bemis was not surprised that she guessed at his presence without looking up at him. The sharp woodswoman's ears, he knew, had had no trouble in identifying his familiar step, afar off. Her claim that she had heard him leave his two-mile-distant home he recognized as part of the buncombe wherewith she maintained her neighborhood prestige as a witch and clairvoyant. Yet, as he slid down the bank an imp of mischief made him reply:

"I come from over Halifax way, auntie. I spent the night there. I haven't been home for a day. You must of heern bitter good if you—"

"*En luxe!*" ("that's a lie"), she responded, her voice shrilling with displeasure at his flippancy. "I heard when you left your door. You and your *honder*," with a nod of contempt at the three black curs that were slipping cautiously down the bank in their master's wake.

Bemis laughed good-naturedly and seated himself on the stone door-sill while Auntie Groot went into the house to pour the thick batter on an iron slab that had been heating on her tumble-down range.

The dogs sniffed curiously about the littered doorway. Then, at a grunt from their owner, they lay down amid the muddy clutter of garbage, and fell a-drowsing in the early sunlight.

Bemis did not speak, nor did Auntie Groot, until the cakes were baked. She dumped them into a wooden trencher and set them on the doorstone beside her guest. Next she brought forth a corncob-corked bottle, half full of molasses, and a chunk of fat salt pork. With this feast between them on the stone, she and Tully began to eat.

In silence they bolted their food, shoulders hunched forward, heads bent over the meal, jaws working noisily. When they had finished, the woman scooped together the fragments that remained and tossed them to the dogs, which gulped the fare scarce more wolfishly than had the two humans.

Auntie Groot fumbled in her pocket and drew forth her corncob pipe and a nearly full paper of rank tobacco. Tully produced his own smoking materials of a like sort, lighting his pipe and then passing the match to his hostess. For a minute or so they smoked without speaking. Then Bemis asked, abruptly:

"Ever hear of Colonel Hardin—young Bruce Hardin's gret-granther?"

The old woman sneered in elaborate contempt, the lip motion revealing a mouth all but barren of teeth.

"*Heer, ja!*" she said. "He sent my father to the jail in Hackensack for taking two of his sheep during the Black Winter. And my uncle burned five of his stacks for it, and hamstrung his two best mules. My uncle would have done more, for he was a man. But he was tracked and they sent him to the jail with my father. It was when I was a girl. But often they spoke of it. Hardin died while they were in the

[96]

jail. He was past ninety. He died. So they could not pay him as they wished. Why do you ask if I heard of him?"

"Because he left a writing that tells all about your granther Groot's treasure," answered Bemis, speaking with elaborate carelessness, yet eying her keenly. "I been reading it."

The old woman's face did not change. Her Indian ancestry stood her in good stead. But her claw-fingers closed tight and then relaxed slowly. Bemis was watching her eyes, not her hands.

"*En luxe!*" she scoffed. "Child, must you still be a fool about a treasure that never was? It has made you *zwak!* I have warned you. I have scolded you. I have told you that you lose money when you leave your still to get rusted while you hunt the hills for what is not there and was never there. You need not scowl at me, child. I have no fear of you. My devil is stronger than your devil. I am not one of the mountain folk who run when you scowl. I tell you there is no treasure. I have told you so fifty times."

"And more'n fifty times I've told you there is," he retorted. "One of these days I aim to find it. I know it's somewheres or other up here, between Pompton and Ringwood. If a mangy Hessian swine had the sense to hide it, I got the sense to find it."

"If you have the sense to find what was never there, go on looking till your whisky still rots away and they put you in the poorhouse," exhorted Auntie Groot. "You're *zwak* about it. Happen you'll remember the first day you came here to my house. You were a brat no higher than your knee is. The other children up here always ran away when they saw me. They do it, right now, and they did it before ever you were born. They will do it when you are dead. But you came up to my hut as bold as brass, and you said you were looking for treasure and you'd heard my granther had owned part of it and you wanted me to tell you where he hid it. I was for scalding you or cutting the skin off your back with my whip. But you looked up at me and I saw your devil behind those ugly black eyes of yours. And I saw if you had no sense, you had no fear, neither. So I gave you food, and I let you come here, after that, for food, and I listened to your talk and you made me laugh. I told you then there was no treasure. I tell you so every time you are here. Stop being a fool and go back to your whisky-making. There is treasure in that."

"I've heard tell, from the Blue-eyed Niggers, that 'Lenape' is the Injun word for two-tongued," observed Bemis, who had waited patiently for the oft-heard harangue to end. "Your gammer was a Lenape, wa'n't she? Old Groot's squaw, I mean. Huh?"

"I let you come here," said the old woman, quietly. "I give you food and I have done many things for you. I like you much, child; you are all that is left for me to like. But that don't give you a lief to spit on the name of my gammer. Besides, I know who she was and I know who was her dad and her mother. *You* don't know who was your granther or your gammer or even your real father."

Tully grinned, in no way offended. Family trees, among the Jackson Whites, are too much like blackberry tangles for umbrage to be taken at slurs on them.

"Go easy!" he urged, to forestall one of the old woman's gusty rages. "Nobody's knocking your folks. And maybe you're saying the truth when you keep telling me you don't b'lieve there was ever any treasure, or maybe you ain't. I've puzzled a heap over that, and I can't rightly make up my mind. But whether you're telling truth or lying to me, I know blame well you haven't any idee where it's hid. I've figgered out that much, these past twenty years of talking to you. If you knew you wouldn't be living up here, half starven, like you do. That's dead sure. But if you'd ever tell me what you *do* know about it—things you've maybe heard old Groot say about it when you were a kid—well, maybe I c'd get a line on how to find it. If I did, you'd get a big piece of it, for your help."

"If you found it," she mocked, "I never would see you again. Not till you got it all spent and came back here to hide out from the folks you'd be owing to. I know that much. If I knew anything about it, I wouldn't tell you, just for that reason. And you know well that I don't know. That is all."

"You've told me you remember old man Groot," insisted Bemis. "A million times you've told me how you took care of him, here in this house he built, after all the rest of his folks and your own folks had died and when he was so old he couldn't stir. You and him must 'a' lived here all alone together till you was pretty near twenty years old, before he died. In that time he must 'a' jawed a heap about old days and the like of that. He *must*. Didn't he ever say about the treasure at all?"

"He told me he had spent most of his time in explaining to curious *uitlanders* that there hadn't ever been any treasure," she snapped. "I've told you that. He used to talk about the old days in Hesse-Cassel and about how he and his friends were sold like so many sheep to the Britishers, to

[99]

fight their wars for them, and how his big brother and his father and Rahl, their chief, were killed at a place called Trenton, by King Washington, one Christmas night. He told me how he and his messmates, Devries and Mann, found chance to run away from the army, after a fight, and how they hid up here."

"But——"

"He was the youngest, my granther," rambled on the crone. "Not much more than a boy he was. He lived after the two others had been long dead. All that he told me. And all that I have told you till I am sick of telling it. Then, when he was an old man, some fool down in the Pomptons heard a made-up story of treasure. Folk used to come up here and torment granther by asking about it. For years they came asking, until he swore at them and drove them off from his house. Is it likely that three soldiers would have treasure in their pockets, when they did not even get pay from the Britishers who had hired them from their master in Hesse-Cassel? It is foolish."

"I told you," said Bemis, when she stopped, breathless from her long oration—"I told you I read a writing by Colonel Hardin. I read it last night. I heard tell about it yesterday. That teacher woman blabbed about it and I went to Hardin's house and I got it. It says those three Hessian fellers were part of a guard that had charge of a pay-chest and a lot of other cash, and they out and run, after a battle, and they sneaked up here with it and buried it. Granther Groot ever gabble to you about *that?*"

He had saved his best shot for the last. But it went wild. By way of reply, Auntie Groot laughed, as in evident relish of a good joke.

[100]

"It is the breed of story old Hardin would tell," she cackled. "He was a liar and he was wide known for a liar. My father used to say Hardin could lie faster than lightning could strike. My mother said the same. If that is where the story about the treasure comes from——"

She finished the sentence with a shoulder shrug and with another laugh of senile merriment.

Bemis glowered at the ground before him. He could not but believe the genuineness of her derision. He knew, too, that her memory was flawless, in spite of her great age. If Colonel Hardin had had the name for being the neighborhood liar, she would have heard of it and would have remembered it.

Tully's air-castles were crumbling about him. If, indeed, the whole rumor of buried Hessian treasure was based on the colonel's word, and if the colonel were notoriously untruthful and given to spinning bascless yarns, for his own amusement——

Years agone, Bemis had heard old people revamp tales of how Auntie Groot's half-breed father had gone down into the Valley and married a young district school-teacher and brought her back to the paternal cabin to rear his brood of quarter-breed youngsters, of whom Auntie Groot was the youngest. Mountaineers said it was from this educated mother that auntie had picked up the ways of talk which, to them, seemed meticulously elegant. They said also that the teacher had been boarding at the Hardin house when, against her host's vehement warnings, she had thrown her future away by marrying the handsome young Hessian-Lenape. In that case, she surely would have been qualified to know whether or not the colonel was untruthful.

"You say your ma called him a liar, too?" he queried.

"My mother did not use the words I use," primly corrected the old woman. "She was born a lady. But she used to say that if Colonel Hardin said the sun was shining, she hunted for her raincloak. She said he told falsehoods for the love of it and to play jokes on his neighbors. That is all I know of it. But it would have been a fine joke for him to have set all the Valley to digging for gold that never had been mined. It is much like many of the jokes my mother used to say he loved to play. If he wrote that there was treasure, it was for all to read. For my mother said that in the old days letters were few and they were passed from hand to hand, for months. It was a good way to spread his joke."

Tully Bemis got slowly to his feet, his giant limbs seeming heavy and unwieldy in the unwonted apathy which had settled down upon him. From childhood he had dreamed of this treasure. Over and over again he had pictured to himself the glorious life he would lead, once he should find it.

Day after day, year after year, the craving had been hot and hotter upon him, forming the sole food for a preternaturally vivid imagination, until it had become a veritable monomania.

For this cause he had curried favor with Auntie Groot until the shrewish old dame had come to care for him as for a loved son. For this cause he had put in thousands of spare hours roaming every cranny and ridge of the Ramapo Mountains, searching, sounding, digging. From infancy he had heard the Hessian treasure talked of, among the Jackson Whites, as an undoubtable reality.

Now, in a handful of words, Auntie Groot had shown him

the fallacy of his dreams. His mind and his imagination raced blindly and aimlessly, like panic-stricken lost dogs. His dark face was a foolish blank. His mighty body sagged, like a paralytic's. His beady black eyes were dull, expressionless.

The old woman was watching him intently. Into her leathern visage of a thousand wrinkles crept a softening expression of pity. Almost timidly she reached out a claw-like hand and petted his arm.

"Child," she said, her shrill voice husky and kind, "I have done much for you, first and last. I may yet do much more for you. But to-day I have done most for you if I have cleared your head of that treasure foolishness. If there had been treasure, it would have done you harm to find it. You would have gone to smash and I would have lost you. You are not the kind to spend wealth wisely. You would be like a baby that drives a runaway horse. Now go back to your still. There is treasure in whisky. You can sell it for what you want to charge, these days. Come back to me for anything I can do. *Var je wal.*"

She turned back into the cabin, gathering up the rudimentary breakfast utensils as she went, and left him standing there, slack-jawed. When she came out again she saw him plodding dully along the ridge crest, the three black dogs trailing after him.

Homeward he bent his lagging steps. His first action when he reached his shack was to take up the two loam-flecked pick-axes that stood in a corner of the wall and to heave them both, with all his strength, down the hillside into a thicket of mountain laurel. By this mute deed he said farewell to his high dreams of wealth.

[103]

THE FAITH OF A COLLIE

Then, body and emotions alike exhausted, he stretched himself out sprawlingly on his bed and slept like a dead man. Nature was taking toll for a sleepless night and for the collapse of life hopes.

CHAPTER

8

THE sun was in the western heavens when he woke with a groan and a cavernous yawn. For a minute or two he lay moveless, staring vaguely up at the grimed ceiling. Something had happened, something hideously unpleasant, but for the instant he could not recall what it might be.

So it is with every son of Eve, some time in life. Misfortune crashes down. Sleep brings brief surcease from mind torture. At the first moment of awakening the brain is mercifully clear of sorrow. Then, at once, comes the formless sensation that something is horribly amiss. And, as with Tully Bemis, memory is swift to snatch up the torture implements.

Bemis sat up sharply as full recollection rushed in on him. Long he sat, puckered of brow and with working lips.

Then he got to his feet and shook himself angrily, as though casting off the garment of dead depression that covered his soul. Back into his mind, braced by sleep, crawled the ghost of hope.

Perhaps Auntie Groot had been fooling him when she said old Colonel Hardin was a lying practical joker. Much more probable was it that, for once, the colonel might have told the truth in that letter to his wife. Bemis remembered now that the letter had enjoined silence on her about the treasure. That did not sound like a joke or like an effort to disseminate the news. He had told his wife he wanted to be the first to hunt for the hoard.

Tully felt hope cease to crawl and begin to rush. Then came reaction. Perhaps the old liar's wife had been a tattletale, a woman who blabbed broadcast about everything that was told her. Bemis knew of such women. Perhaps her husband bade her be silent on this theme, in the knowledge that such a command would make her the more avid to tell the supposed secret.

Then Bemis laughed at this new doubt, as fantastic. From his recollection of the letter, it had been written as in good faith. There was still a chance—an increasingly strong chance—that the treasure was a fact and not a myth.

Reviving hope made the man realize he was hungry, also that he had planned to go down to Oakland to-day to lay in provisions. His larder was all but empty.

At any other time he would have gone to his nearest Jackson White neighbor and commandeered enough food of sorts to tide him over until the morrow. But in his present nervous mood of alternating hope and misery he did not want to mix with his neighbors and listen to their obsequious chatter. It would be simpler to walk down to Oakland and buy the stock of provisions he needed, as he had planned to.

As he set forth, the three black dogs sprang up from their resting-places in the shade and trotted forward to join him. Gruffly he ordered them back. He could not take his curs into the villages of the valley. Down there they had fool laws about the licensing of dogs. Unless a man chose to pay out a whole dollar for a measly little copper tag with a number on it, his dogs would be impounded and he must needs pay good money to get them free again.

While Tully felt confident of his own easy ability to protect his mongrels against any dog-catcher or against any two dog-catchers, yet these officials had the law behind them. They could stir up trouble. As long as the dog-catchers kept on their own territory and did not come up into the mountains to enforce the license law, Bemis and others of his kind deemed it wisest to meet the courtesy halfway by keeping their dogs outside of village limits.

Wherefore, to-day Tully ordered his trio of black satellites back into the dooryard, and he proceeded down the mountain alone.

He chose the shortest trail, if the steepest. As he came to the foot of a ledge, where two overgrown paths converged, he halted at sound of pebbles rattling down the far side.

Looking up, he saw Horace Bladen descending the hill by means of the second path. Bladen was still fifty feet away from him and something like twenty feet above him. He did not look down, but strolled along, studying something he held in his palm.

Over his shoulder swung his worn black bag. In his

belt was stuck his geological hammer. He seemed highly elated, if one might judge by the half-smile of triumph on his face and the gay excitement in the eyes which beamed from behind the huge horn spectacles.

Bemis, from below, noted the geologist's exultant bearing, and he wondered. He had profound contempt for the lanky convalescent who spent his days pottering around among the rocky hills, chipping daintily at stones and squinting at them through a funny round glass or pouring the contents of little bottles on them.

Most of the mountaineers were inclined to believe Horace mildly insane. Bemis had begun to share the opinion. At first, Tully had watched with glum uneasiness the geologist's daily wanderings through the mountains. Bladen seemed always searching for something.

Jealous lest another be on the track of the treasure, Tully had devoted the best part of a week to stalking the scientist, following him wherever he wandered, spying craftily upon him. At the end of that time Bemis was satisfied that the idiot was, for some reason, more interested in the rocks themselves than in anything which might be buried among them. So he gave up his espionage, satisfied that Horace had no designs on the hoard.

Now, however, a twinge of the olden doubt seeped back upon him. Why in blue blazes should a man look as jubilant as this wontedly glum-faced and lantern-jawed lunatic, unless he had found something to thrill him out of his usual melancholy?

Wherefore, instead of continuing on his journey downhill or declaring his presence, Tully Bemis shrank instinctively back into the mountain laurel clump behind him. With the stealthy noiselessness of a snake he moved, his giant body making no rustling sound among the crisp leafage. Back he stepped until a hazel copse gave him the shelter he wished. Then he came to a crouching halt and peered upward through the leaves and twigs toward the slowly descending Bladen.

A born mountaineer, Bemis had long since learned the difficult art of moving through dense woods without betraying his presence by so much as a snapping twig. It is the art of the woodsman and the trapper, and almost impossible for a town-bred man to attain.

Why he should have taken shelter at this time Bemis did not try to reason out. Like many of his acts, it was done by animal instinct. Something in Bladen's face and bearing had caught his attention and his curiosity.

That was all. And he proceeded to watch the geologist, from cover, while Horace came down the steep ledge path with his usual cautious slowness.

Arrived at the patch of level ground at the ledge's foot, Bladen paused for a few seconds. Now that he did not have to calculate his steps down the uncertain and precipitous bit of ledge trail, he could give greater attention to the object in his hand at which he had been staring so ecstatically when Bemis first saw him from below.

Crane his thick neck as he would and strain his keen eyes as he might, Tully was not able to see what Bladen held in his cupped palm. It might be a half dozen gold pieces. It might be a huge diamond, such as the man in that picture play over at Pompton Lakes found in an African mine. It might be anything.

Assuredly it was something of great value, from the

way Horace was gloating over it. There could be no doubt of that. A treasure-hunter himself, Bemis yearned to see what thing of wealth Bladen had found this day among the Ramapos. Almost was he tempted to take a step from his hiding-place to try to get a glimpse at it.

Better still, he could slouch forward, as if coming from somewhere along the mountain-side, and hail the geologist casually and ask what he was looking at. That would be best. He was about to come forth in the most casual manner he could summon up, when he heard other and lighter steps coming down the same trail that Bladen had taken.

Tully checked his own forward motion and stayed where he was. He recognized the steps. Sibyl Gates was coming home, by this route, from her day at school. She and Bladen were friends. Bladen had rescued her, just the other day, from Roan Shively. In picture shows, when a fellow rescued a girl, he married her. Maybe she and Bladen were sweethearts.

In any event, it was certain Horace would blab to her about this mysterious thing he had found. Tully was well within hearing.

And now Bladen heard the steps, too. He looked up toward the top of the ledge where the path came over the crest. He did not hide the unseen object he was holding in his palm. Good! That meant he would tell her about it.

At the ledge-top appeared Sibyl, the big gold-red collie beside her. Bemis was grateful he had left his dogs at home. Now no unbidden growl or bark could betray his presence.

At sight of Bladen looking up at her, Sibyl waved gayly to him. Mars started down the steep few yards of ledge path to greet him.

[110]

Bladen answered the girl's salutation by shouting exultantly to her:

"Nine loud cheers for ME! I've found treasure in the Ramapos! Gold! *Gold!* GOLD!"

Sibyl had started down the steep ten-foot slope of the ledge path, the great collie picking his dainty way amid the rubble close behind her.

At Bladen's triumph shout of "Gold! *Gold!* GOLD!" she stopped short, in sheer astonishment.

Now it is not well nor safe to come to an unbalanced abrupt halt, midway down such an incline, more especially if rubble or pebbles chance to strew the path. Sibyl's feet checked their momentum; the rest of her did not. She strove to regain her balance. A round pebble turned under the ball of her foot.

The girl pitched forward, helpless to avert a fall.

Bladen, a few feet below, saw her predicament and jumped forward up the yard or so of intervening path. As she lurched forward he caught her in his arms, her slender weight all but upsetting the none-too-strong geologist.

For an instant he held her thus, striving with might and main to retain his own footing. Completely off balance, Sibyl had no recourse but to cling to him, her arms close about his stringy throat. In the collision his spectacles were knocked off. But, subconsciously, he kept his grip on the object he had been holding up for her inspection.

All this Tully Bemis saw. From the thicket, the whole scene was as visible to him as Bladen's words had been audible. Dumfounded, his brain afire at what he had heard, he crouched there.

As he stared he saw Sibyl apparently leap forward into

the arms that were flung forth to her. He saw man and maid clasped in a rapturous and prolonged embrace. From where he hid he could not note that Sibyl's impetuous forward motion was caused by a loss of balance, nor that Bladen had merely caught her in his arms to keep her from a dangerous fall among the rocks.

To Bemis this was the ecstatic meeting of two adoring and adored lovers—an embrace as romantically effusive as anything he had seen in the movies. It admitted of only one interpretation to him. Bladen and Sibyl were sweethearts. Evidently it was through love, not chivalry alone, that Howard had rescued her from Roan Shively. The two were lovers.

Now this patent fact held something like a million per cent less than no interest at all to Tully. He was not concerned in any way with the amours of these interloping outlanders.

But he was more concerned and stirred over one phase of the scene than over anything that had come into his life. His blood was aboil and his heart was racing. His brain whirled with the unbelievable tidings Horace had called so gayly to his sweetheart.

The geologist had announced that he had found the treasure! He had shouted of gold!

Yes, Bemis knew he himself had been right in his own earlier suspicions of the scientist. Bladen had been prowling the Ramapos in quest of the treasure. And now he had found it!

Probably he had been guided thereto by some chart left by Colonel Hardin—a chart he carried with him on his hunt, and which Tully, therefore, had not been able to find in his wholesale looting of all the written matter in Bruce Hardin's house.

This turtle-necked city cuss had come to the mountains and had grabbed away the Hessian treasure from under Tully Bemis's grasp! Tully's amaze merged into homicidal fury.

He tensed his muscles for a spring upon the treasure-finder. He would wrench from him that handful of gold coin he was holding! By tortures he would make him tell where the cache was that contained the rest of it. In Bemis's giant hands the geologist would be as a baby.

Never mind about the law which Bladen might invoke against him, with the girl for witness! Before the state police could find him, in those mountain mazes, he would have collected the mass of treasure and fled far beyond their reach. Besides—why need anyone set the law on him? It would be pitiably easy to strangle man and woman both, and hide them where they could never be found. There were a score of such places. First, Bladen should be made to locate the cache for him. Then——

As Bladen stepped back to level ground and set Sibyl safely on her feet, Mars followed her to the patch of flat rock below the descent. All this in the moment wherein Bemis had recovered from his daze and laid his sudden plan of violence.

Now, as Tully braced himself for his leap, the collie lifted his chiseled nostrils and sniffed suspiciously. Bemis was enough of a dog man to read the action aright. Though the breeze was blowing from the wrong direction, yet the

[113]

collie had scented vaguely an alien presence. In another few seconds he would cast about to locate it.

Bemis was unarmed. A weaponless man is none too good a match for a charging seventy-pound collie. The giant hesitated. Into his memory flashed Bruce Hardin's warning words, repeated by the beaten Roan Shively. Bruce had told the Shivelys that Bladen always carried the same pistol wherewith he menaced Roan. Also that Horace was a dead shot.

It is one thing to launch oneself on an unprepared victim, and quite another thing to be attacked by a savage dog and then to be shot down by a crack marksman. With Mars to give the alarm and to impede Tully's rush, Bladen would have ample time to draw that pistol of his and to turn the tables on his assailant before they could come to grips.

Horace might even march him to the Oakland lock-up at pistol-point, should Tully hazard such an attack. Then farewell to all hope of getting the treasure. Warned, Bladen would be certain to remove it before Bemis could get free.

No, this was no time to carry out his golden plan. More resolved than ever to seize the hoard from its finder, yet Tully knew he must find another way to do it.

As silently as a snake he drew back through the thicket, moving fast, yet without the visible stirring of a twig. Around the jut of the hillcliff he worked his rapid way. Forty yards farther on he came to another of the innumerable precipice ledges. It was directly beneath him. Lowering himself over the side, he dropped to the next rock-plateau, some nine feet beneath and made his way faster and with less caution around its curved face, to a path a furlong beyond.

He was barely in time. As he had foreseen, Mars began to cast about. Presently the collie caught the scent of the man he sought. Following it at a hand gallop through the undergrowth, he came presently to the ledge over whose side Bemis had dropped. There, of course, the trail ended, though the scent still hung elusive in the air.

CHAPTER

9

MARS cast about vainly, along the ledge crest, in an effort to pick it up again. Then, worried and growling softly, he pattered back to Sibyl and Bladen. They had been too engrossed to notice his brief wanderings at all.

"Oh, I'm sorry I was so awkward!" Sibyl had exclaimed, disengaging herself from Bladen's angular clasp. "It was clever of you to catch me. If you hadn't——"

"If I hadn't," supplemented Horace, peering nearsightedly about for his fallen spectacles, "the worst you'd have incurred would have been a tumble into a bottomless abyss almost five feet deep. Your rather pretty nose might have been bumped and you might even have gotten a sprained wrist. That is the sum total of the disaster I saved you from."

THE FAITH OF A COLLIE

"I feel like the perpetually rescued maiden in the old-fashioned novels or the moving pictures," she laughed, straightening her hair. "First you save me from Roan Shively at the muzzle of a geological hammer, and now you catch me in my fall from a misses'-and-children's-size cliff. Pretty soon, at this rate, the small boys at the back of the theater gallery will begin to clap every time the film shows you appearing on the horizon when I am in any predicament. . . . What on earth are you doing?" she broke off, as he sank on both knees and proceeded to examine the rocky and leaf-strewn ground at their feet.

"I am enacting the heroic rôle of spectacles-retriever," he said, solemnly, rising with the recovered glasses in one hand and with the other still clenched. "See, neither lens was broken. That is an unusual reward of knight-errantry. The lenses cost three dollars and seventy-five cents each. Either one is of greater cash value than the treasure I discovered to-day. I——"

"The treasure!" she cried. "Oh, I remember now! You called out to me that you had found gold. I was so excited I lost my balance. And that flustered me so badly that I forgot all about the gold. Is it a joke?"

"A joke?" he repeated, indignantly. "Every geological paper in America and Europe will tell about it. I shall be almost famous. It is the most interesting discovery I have made yet. Look!"

He opened his clenched hand and displayed a few flakes of lightish stone, shot with dull yellowish specks.

"What is it?" she asked, looking at the particles he exhibited so proudly. "More antimony or——?"

"Antimony?" he scoffed. "Compared with this, the finding of antimony traces was a mere nothing. Do you know what this is? But of course you wouldn't. You waste years in mastering the silly classics and higher mathematics and you neglect the most fascinating study on earth—the study of geology. All of you are like that."

"Now that I have been duly rebuked," she said, meekly, "suppose you tell me what this uninteresting-looking stuff is, that has excited you so and made you sing a chant about 'Gold! *Gold!* GOLD!' It doesn't look like anything to me. It——"

"It is treasure," he contradicted, in reproof. "Real treasure. It is the most remarkable find any American geologist has made in years. These specimens are true foliate tellurium!"

"Wonderful!" she exclaimed, in mock astonishment. "Magnificent! And now can any little boy or girl in the sound of my voice tell me what 'foliate tellurium' means? *I* can't, for one. What is it?"

"It is one of the most bountiful matrices of gold," he lectured. "It is found plentifully in Transylvania and in several parts of Australia. Strong traces of it even have been located near Red Cloud, Colorado, and in Calaveras County, California. But Emmins and Richthal and other authorities have declared that it is totally absent elsewhere in the United States—certainly east of the Mississippi River. Well, right here in the Ramapo Mountains of northern New Jersey I have found two distinct specimens. I found it in a flaw of——"

"And there is really gold in it?" she asked, in real interest.

"Yes," he said, less buoyantly. "In Australia and, they

[118]

say, even in Red Cloud, the content ranges from five to nine per cent gold. Judging by these specimens—at a rough guess, of course, and before any effort to assay—I should estimate the gold-content as only about one-half of one per cent. Still, that makes the discovery none the less——"

" 'One-half of one per cent,' " she repeated, in mischievous disregard of his eagerness. "That has a familiar sound. Doesn't the phrase occur somewhere in the Volstead Act? I seem to have heard it."

Observing his chagrin at her levity, she asked:

"But does that mean there is really gold in these mountains, Mr. Bladen?"

"Gold!" he scoffed, impatiently. "Of course there is. There is gold everywhere. In sea water, in a thousand varieties of rock, in soil, in river beds—everywhere. Science says lately that quicksilver can be electrified into yielding particles of gold. There is gold in every state in the Union. The only trouble is that it occurs in such minute particles that it would cost ten times its value to extract it. For instance, these specimens of foliate tellurium don't contain enough gold particles to have any commercial value. The chances are that they are freaks and that there is not a pound, troy, of foliate tellurium in the entire Ramapo range. But that does not make the discovery any less important. The North Pole is worthless; as a real estate proposition or as a farming region. Yet Peary won immortality by discovering it. It will be somewhat the same with me, when I establish my claim to this——"

"I'm sorry I was so unsympathetic about it," she apologized. "I see now how much it means to you. When you

[119]

told me you had found the treasure, I was foolish enough to suppose you meant the Hessian pay-chest and the treasure-casket that Mr. Hardin read us about, in old Colonel Hardin's letter. That's why I was so excited and why I didn't enthuse more when you explained. I'm sorry. But when you shouted 'GOLD!' I——"

"I mean it," he declared. "There is more gold of high quality in these two flakes of tellurium than in any rock substance of fifty times its volume in the state of New Jersey! It is a genuine gold discovery, and it is just as remarkable a discovery from a science viewpoint as if the metal had been found in practicable bulk. . . . I am a crank, on my own profession," he finished, shame-facedly. "I'm sorry I was so blatant about it. But you see you were the first person I happened to meet, after I found it, half an hour ago. I was on my way home to write my report of it for the *Geological Monthly* and then to embody it in my book when you——"

"When I fell into your arms and then was too stupid to fall into your enthusiasm," she supplemented. "Tell me more about it."

Tully Bemis abandoned his idea of going to Oakland for provisions. His mind in a red turmoil, he went back by roundabout way to his own home. His brain was fever-hot, his pulses were singing, a raging mania possessed him.

All his life he had dreamed of the Hessian treasure. Waking and sleeping, the lure of it had been upon him. He had envisioned it in myriad forms. Now as a huge steel chest piled high with glittering British gold pieces, now as a casket of shimmering many-colored jewels; but always he had visioned it as belonging to himself, as being found by him, as being lavished and reveled in and squandered in luxury by him.

Auntie Groot, by her tale of Colonel Hardin's lack of truth, had dashed his spirits to the dust. He had felt his life hopes dead within him. Then, as he was trying to force himself to hope again, he had heard Horace Bladen's jubilant announcement that the treasure had been found.

Hot upon his first homicidal fury at the finder now followed a wild exultance that the tale of the Hessian hoard was true and that the treasure at last had been unearthed. Bladen had held in his palm a specimen of it.

From Horace's yell of "GOLD!" Bemis conjectured that the treasure was in the form of a chestful of gold pieces and that Bladen was bringing a handful of these back to the valley to prove his discovery.

On the morrow, of course, Bladen and Bruce Hardin and perhaps more of the smugly law-abiding valley farmers would come up into the mountains, with canvas bags, and maybe with wheelbarrows as well, and clean out the treasure-chest and casket, and carry their precious contents down to the Pompton Lakes bank, for safe keeping.

Probably the treasure was so heavy that it would take several men to carry it. Groot and Devries and Mann had been reputed strong. Yet they had had all they could do, the three of them, to get it up into the mountains.

A spindling man like Bladen could not possibly carry it down to the valley, alone. So, instead of loading his pockets with as much as he could stagger under, the poor simp had taken only a few gold pieces in one hand to show to his friends, so that they could come up there with him, next day, and get the rest of it.

His friends! The bespectacled fool probably would tell everyone. By to-morrow the mountains might be thick with valley men. Bladen was going to tell! He was going to make it possible for others to share his wealth. He had begun by blithering about it to the girl he was in love with. A man who would yell such a secret to a woman would squall it to the whole world!

A gust of murderous contempt swept over Bemis, strangling and suffocating him. Then by sheer force of will he forced himself to a strange calm. Once more his mountaineer brain began to function with its wonted craftiness, spurred on now by his irresistible urge for the treasure.

The sun was low. That meant the treasure-finder would not be able to lead his friends up into the mountains to-night to bear home the hoard. The way was long and there was no moon. It would be hazardous for any non-mountaineer to try to traverse those deceptive ridges in the dark.

Moreover, Bladen would not know that any of the Jackson Whites was aware of his discovery. He would not see any need of haste or for caution. He would figure there was plenty of time and the treasure was safe from chance discovery that night by anyone else.

He would organize his expedition; and he and Bruce Hardin and the others would climb the mountains to-morrow morning on their exhilarating task of lugging sacks of gold down into the valley.

The valley! How Tully Bemis hated the very name of

the rich farm region! It was peopled by folk who grubbed in the soil for a living, who wore clean clothes on Sundays, who shaved regularly and who took baths, who banked their money, who led adventureless and stupidly honest lives. It was the abode of the Law—the Law which once had jailed him and once had sent him to hiding for weary months, far from his loved Ramapos. The valley was the symbol of all he loathed and feared.

And now from the valley had come a lanky spectacled city cuss who had found a way to make the mountains reveal to him their hundred-and-forty-year-old secret, and who had discovered the treasure—the treasure a better man had spent twenty years of his life hunting for!

Again the murder lust flamed and swirled hot in Bemis's heart, and again he choked it back, forcing himself to clear thought.

They would come to-morrow morning, probably soon after sunrise. Well, Tully had until then to block them and to force Bladen to tell him just where the hoard was cached. Twelve full hours or more—if only he could make use of the time.

He stood, head bent, chest heaving, forming plan after plan, and rejecting each as fast as it was made.

Most of all he craved to creep to the Hardin house after all had gone to bed, to steal into Bladen's room, there, after gagging him, to torture him into revealing where the treasure was.

No, he might lie. It would be better to gag him or knock him on the head and then lug him off, over one shoulder, to the hills, and, by dint of certain olden Indian devices

[123]

Auntie Groot had once told him about, to make Bladen lead him to the very spot where the hoard awaited its rightful master.

This idea appealed strongly to Tully. It was simple. It was certain. . . . No, it was neither certain nor simple!

The dog! That big hairy brute of a collie! From divers Jackson Whites, who took a more than neighborly interest in the valley farmers' chickens, Bemis had heard fearsome tales of Mars's prowess as a watch-dog.

Tully knew, on second thought, that Mars was sure to give the alarm before the intruder could come within a hundred feet of the Hardin house, and that the collie would sally forth to the assault. True, there were means of silencing forever even the most doughty watch-dog, but not before his barking should have waked the household.

If only there were more time! If only there were a single day wherein Bemis could leave poisoned meat in tempting reach of Mars as the collie should accompany Sibyl to or from school! Or if only this kidnapping of Bladen could be achieved during the daytime, while Mars was absent in the mountains! It had been ridiculously easy to rob Hardin, in the dog's absence, the day before.

But what was to be done must be done to-night, if ever. To-morrow would be too late. There was no time to arrange preliminaries. There was no hope of kidnapping Bladen.

All at once the deep furrows between Tully's eyes vanished. The man stood upright, eager and tense. His problem was solved!

Not by mere chance had he attained his mental ascendancy over the degenerate mountaineers who were his neighbors. Not by chance had he wiggled a dozen times out of the closing nets of the law. Not by chance had he maintained his moonshine whisky still, at a big profit and without suspicion from the authorities. The brain which had accomplished all this had just hit upon a cleverer and more daring scheme than any of its predecessors.

Swinging across to his widowed brother's shack, a quarter-mile away, he sent his nephew, Cleppy, on three successive errands, each message being couched in the cryptic jargon of the mountains. The third message alone he committed to writing. This was to Auntie Groot. The superstitious Cleppy took the note in terror and ran with shaking legs to deliver it. He and all the rest of the Jackson White children dreaded unspeakably to venture near the ancient brown woman's cabin, especially when, as now, night was coming on.

Ethan Wallace and his wife spent part of the evening with Hardin. The farmer had come across to arrange final details about the tractor they were to rent jointly.

He and his wife had wanted Sibyl to join them, but she was busy, working out her next month's school schedule, along lines forwarded to her that day by the society which employed her. When this cabalistic theme should be mastered, she had still all her class's monthly examination papers to correct. So, reluctantly, she refused, and settled herself in the living-room, under the one lamp, the table in front of her piled high with smudgy penciled papers and prim textual charts.

She had been working for perhaps a half-hour when there was a knock at the door. She opened it, admitting Bruce Hardin.

"I ought to say I'm sorry to break in on your profound

scholastic labors," he hailed her, "but I'm not. Wallace said he left the tractor manual on his kitchen table and forgot to bring it over. So I brought up some point that, presumably, only the manual could decide. I volunteered to run over here and get it for him. Here I am."

He sat down, uninvited. The girl asked, in some surprise:

"But aren't you going to get the manual?"

"Oh yes," he made answer, "I'll get it presently. It is a hard thing to find. I am looking everywhere for it now. In a few minutes I'll remember he said it's in the kitchen, on the corner of the table. Then I'll get it and take it back to him. Meanwhile——"

"Meanwhile," Sibyl reminded him, trying not to smile at his impudence—"meanwhile, I have my chart to study and then these examination papers to correct. To-day we held our solemn monthly examinations, up at the school, you know."

Bruce reached across and picked up two or three of the crumpled ruled sheets from the heap. At the top of one he read the caption, in Sibyl's neat hand, "*History.*" Question No. 1 was: "Who discovered America, and when?" With some difficulty he spelled out the ensuing reply to the query, an answer scrawled laboriously by one Dode Wyble:

"*It is diskvred in 8een92 by Cuolmbs but uncle Tice ses thats a dam lie it is diskvred by Gorge Wasngton a cuple of yeers or moar befoar then and uncle Tice aut to no becus he nose evrithin.*"

The girl broke in on Bruce's guffaw of appreciation by begging:

"Don't laugh! You *mustn't!* It isn't funny. It's—it's pathetic. They try so hard! And they have generations of

[126]

blank ignorance behind them. They are groping for——"

"Surely not for soap?" he interjected, gazing at the smudged paper. "Oh, I wish you'd give it all up, Sibyl! Won't you? It'll wear out the soul and the nerve and the enthusiasm of you, soon or late. And you'll have wrecked your gorgeous life without having made any real inroads on their idiocy. It——"

"Well," she challenged, as ever in arms in defense of her loved profession, "suppose I do wear myself out teaching up there? Isn't it splendidly worth while—if I can bring a single glimmer of education or progress or civilization to them? Isn't it? How better could I possibly spend the life God has given me than in——?"

"If you really want to know," said Bruce, leaning forward and speaking with eager impulse, "if you really want to know how you can spend it better, I'll tell you. I——"

"Tell me what?" she asked, wondering at his new depth of earnestness.

"I can tell you how you can spend your life so as to bring more divine happiness and inspiration to *one* man than all the rest of the world can bring. Will you let me tell——?"

He got no further. Indeed, the last words went unheard by the girl. For the coal-scuttle, beside the polished living-room stove, capsized with a resounding crash, followed by a grievous yowl from somewhere beneath it.

The Wallaces' elderly cat—an ill-favored and ugly-tempered and scrawny pinkish-brown, sore-eyed piebald creature—had been asleep on the mantel-shelf above the unlit stove. Her chosen couch was a chenille mat in gay colors which usually served as groundwork for a vase of flowers. The vase had been emptied that day and had not been replaced. The cat had sought the vacant mat as a bed.

Waking, she had yawned and stretched herself. The mat, at this transverse motion, slipped on the white surface of the mantel. The cat had lost her footing and tumbled, landing on the edge of the half-full coal-scuttle and bringing it over on top of her.

Liberally sprinkled with coal dust, she emerged, in one furious bound which carried her to the very center of the table. There, her coal-dusty paws wrought further havoc with such traces of cleanliness as the examination papers might have retained.

Spitting and shaking herself, she glared at Bruce and at Sibyl.

The girl broke into a hysterical laugh. Hardin choked back a word Sibyl would not have cared to hear. Perhaps a man's sense of humor is never quite at its best when some ludicrous happening interrupts his first proposal. Bruce could have wrung the cat's mangy neck with a glad heart.

"Oh dear!" cried Sibyl, checking her laughter as the cat stalked across the rest of the table's papers and jumped to the floor with an indignant bump. "Now she's tracked up all those charts, too! And I've got to send them back to the society, when I've read them! I'll never be able to get that coal dust off them. Isn't it horrid?"

"Next time I meet her in the road, when I have Mars along," he promised, grimly, "I'll see he avenges the smeared charts. As for the examination papers, the addition of a little wholesome coal dust really makes them look cleaner than they were. But I was saying to you that you could——"

[128]

"You mustn't set Mars on her!" insisted Sibyl. "Mr. Wallace would never forgive you. He and Mrs. Wallace love that cat as you love Mars. I don't know why, but they do. She's an atrocious old thing. She is the only animal I ever saw that I couldn't get to liking. I never see her without thinking of Shakespeare's phrase, 'Marvelous ill-favored.' And she has a horrible temper, too. But they are wild about her. They have had her ever since she was born. Think! They actually named her 'Fluffy'! They named her so when she was a little kitten. Did you ever hear of such a name for such a——?"

"Shan't we sidetrack the miserable Fluffy for a while?" urged Bruce. "I never get a minute to see you alone, and I'm not going to let this rare chance get away from me. I——"

"Say, young feller," demanded Wallace from the door-way, "are we paying you a visit this evening or are you paying us one? I only ask because it might be kind of sociabler if we was all of us to be in one house, instead of playing puss-in-the-corner. I thought you came over here to get that manual. We waited till we got sleepy, and then we came back to see what was keeping you. I—— Suffering snakes! Been playing powder-puff, on the table, with coal dust?"

Mrs. Wallace from the door, caught sight of the black paw-marks on her cherished white tablecloth and the coal lumps which radiated across her clean carpet from the collapsed scuttle. Down upon the wreckage she bore, her sense of ill-treatment at the hands of her recent negligent host wiped out by this outrage to housewifely neatness.

THE FAITH OF A COLLIE

Under cover of the chatter Bruce Hardin took his sulky leave. His chance was gone, for the present—snatched from him by a wretched cat.

"By this time," he told himself, glumly, as he plodded home, "I'd have known if she cares or not. Lord! Can I ever get my courage up to the sticking-point again?"

Sibyl turned back to her neglected chart-work after helping her landlady to clear up the scattered coal from the floor. Subconsciously she heard Wallace and his wife discussing Bruce's rudeness in leaving them to cool their heels in his living-room while he sat at ease in theirs.

"It isn't a bit like him," Mrs. Wallace was saying. "What on earth made him do it? Here he'd never even touched the manual! He was just staring at Sibyl, sort of foolish-like. He looked—let's see, now, what was it he reminded me of when we looked in and saw him? He reminded me of something funny. I know that. I—— Why, I remember now! He had just the same queer duck-in-a-thunderstorm look that *you* had, Eth Wallace, the time you asked me to marry you. I——"

She glanced sidewise at Sibyl and said no more. But her prattle had pierced the study-thoughts and had reached the girl's brain. Back to her mind came in a flash the man's expression as he had leaned so impetuously toward her. A wave of crimson rushed to her face. She drew a long trembling breath. Then, with school-teacherly resolve, she set herself to her tasks afresh.

Soon the Wallaces went up to bed, first winding the hall clock and locking the downstairs windows and putting the cat out on the porch for the night. Sibyl worked on. Often she did this on evenings when examination papers had to be

[130]

corrected. To-night she found it increasingly hard to keep her mind on her work and away from the memory of Bruce Hardin's boyishly eager face as it had bent toward her.

At last she finished reading the society's charts, with no clear idea as to what they were about. They must wait until her mind should be more receptive to their wisdom. She reached out for the topmost of the examination sheets— Dode Wyble's history paper which Bruce had laughed at. Picking it up and taking a pencil from the table, she prepared to correct it—a Herculean task by itself.

As she did so the faintest of timid taps sounded on the glass of the window just behind her.

Sibyl turned about, half thinking the noise had been made by some night insect beating against the pane. As she looked she well-nigh exclaimed aloud in startled surprise.

A moon-dim little face was staring in through the window at her—a face framed against the dense darkness of the cloudy night.

Then, focusing her gaze, she recognized the midnight visitor. The face belonged to Cleppy Bemis, the least unpromising of her pupils. The child was ghastly pale and he was trembling. With a shaky forefinger he beckoned to her. Sibyl got up and went to the window to open it, abstractedly thrusting into her belt the pencil and the examination paper as she went. But Cleppy shrank back, again beckoning and then pointing beseechingly toward the side door of the porch, which opened into the living-room.

Wondering what ill-usage at home could have driven the frightened youngster to her for refuge at such an hour, Sibyl went to the side door, unbolted it, and held it invitingly open. The boy shrank back still further from the

[131]

stream of lamplight, one finger to his lips, the forefinger of the other hand still beckoning. At the farthest edge of the porch he paused in his retreat, standing beside the exiled Fluffy.

Amused, pitying, Sibyl stepped out on the porch.

Behind her the house door swung noiselessly shut. She turned, surprised at this phenomenon on a windless night.

On the same instant deft hands pinioned her from behind with a rope. Other hands still more deftly thrust a handkerchief into her spasmodically opened mouth, stifling to silence the unborn cry of terror that sprang to her lips.

CHAPTER

10

THE light from the two living-room windows cast a dimly suffused glow on the end of the porch. Sibyl Gates's eyes focusing to the dimness, the frightened girl was aware of three men standing on the top of the steps where Cleppy Bemis had been beckoning to her. The boy had vanished, swallowed by the darkness from which the three newcomers had appeared.

She could not see either of the two men who had seized and pinioned and gagged her so noiselessly from behind.

In the tumult of terror—as is sometimes the way in times of stark distress—her mind centered for an instant on a trivial, not to say ridiculous, object. She found herself noting that Fluffy, the sore-eyed and disreputable old house cat, had not moved nor shown the slightest interest in this sudden lively bit of action.

[133]

Unconcerned as ever, the cat sat hunched morbidly on her scrap of mat on the porch corner. Fluffy was of a stolid temperament. Nothing short of a cyclone or a pursuing dog, ordinarily, could shake her from her scornful disdain for all the world.

From the time Sibyl had stepped forth from the house in answer to Cleppy's mysterious window-tapping, to the time she stood, trussed and gagged, confronting the three men who loomed vaguely up before her, not five seconds had passed. The intruders had done their work with swift certainty.

One man, of the three at the top of the steps, came softly forward. Even on the creaky porch boards his bare feet seemed shod in silence. He stood a head taller than his two companions, and his shoulders bulked as wide, through the gloom, as steam radiators. Sibyl recognized his silhouette, even before his features waxed dimly recognizable in the faint light.

Somehow her recognition of Tully Bemis served to quell her sudden fright. He was a mortal man. His presence robbed the midnight scene of its first tinge of the supernatural. To her own surprise a calmness took possession of her. Later there would be time for fear, at thought of having fallen into the hands of Tully and his fellow-mountaineers. For the moment, her relief at sight of him gave her a queer steadiness of nerves and set her brain to working normally again, if with an unwonted quickness.

Speaking in a whisper so low that she had to strain her ears to catch the words, Tully leaned down over her and said:

"If you holler or make any racket or try to rassle loose,

I'll have to rap you over the head. If you keep still, there won't any harm come to you. Nod if you mean you'll keep still."

His tone was unruffled. Yet Sibyl had no pleasant illusions that he might be bluffing. She checked her impulse to give forth the muffled cry which should waken the household or to pound a tattoo on the floor with her heels in the hope of bringing Wallace downstairs to investigate. If these men already had risked so much to capture her—if they planned to carry her away—a blow on the temple from Tully's hammer-like fist assuredly would strike her senseless before help could come. In such case he and his men could run off with her on their shoulders and be well out of reach before Ethan Wallace could get downstairs.

"Nod if you mean you'll keep still," repeated Bemis, in the same half-audible whisper.

Sibyl did more than nod. The man who had thrust the ball of cloth into her mouth had withdrawn his hand from her lips as Bemis addressed her. With a violent effort of the tongue the girl thrust forth the wadded handkerchief. Her mind was working with a cool precision which astonished her. In melodramatic junctures one's mentality is prone to be either far above or far below par.

"What do you want of me?" she asked, coolly, her whisper no louder than Tully's own.

Bemis made as though to thrust back the gag. The man behind her also grabbed at it. But, in the same gesture, Tully motioned him to desist. Evidently he inferred from the whisper that Sibyl was taking the affair as he had warned her to.

"You got sense," he whispered, in satisfaction; adding:

[135]

"If you keep still and don't make a fuss, you won't get harmed any. We got to take you somewheres. You'll be let come back here, safe, pretty soon. Now will you go quiet or do I have to lug you over my shoulder? Speak up, and speak up soft. We got no time."

"I will go with you," she made low answer, her voice still calm, yet with a thread of new excitement in it. "I'll go because I have to go. Of course you know you'll go to prison for this, later on, if you're caught. I——"

"I won't git caught," he answered, in grim certainty. "Come on, now. We got no time to——"

"I'll go quietly, and on foot," she continued, unmoved, "on one condition. Grant that condition and I'll go quietly. If you refuse it, I am going to cry out. If you doubt that, refuse what I ask. I don't know where I am going. It will be among strangers, where I'll be lonesome and unhappy. I want to take along my cat, to be a companion for me. I can't bear to go away without her."

"Gee!" grunted Bemis, in relief at the easiness of the condition and in contempt for its silliness. "Is that all? Lug her along if you're a mind to. She looks more like a scarecrow, to me, than a cat. Hustle now."

He signaled to the man who was pinioning her arms to loose his hold. He himself laid a lightly powerful grip on her shoulder.

Sibyl stooped down and gathered the protesting and cranky cat into her arms, holding her closely to prevent her from escaping. Then under the propelling guidance of Tully Bemis's shoulder grasp, she tiptoed off the porch. Ethan Wallace would have marveled at her sudden love for Fluffy.

The two men who had been behind her dropped noiselessly into line with the two who had stood beside Tully. And now, as they flitted stealthily past the bar of light from a window, Sibyl saw that all four were of the Blue-eyed Nigger clan.

Apparently, Roan Shively's merciless thrashing and the printed warning left by Bruce had deterred any of the Jackson Whites from joining the kidnapping expedition. That, or else Tully felt he could rely more completely on the Blue-eyed Niggers' dread of himself and their slavish obedience to Auntie Groot.

Westward across the meadow moved the silent procession, Sibyl in its midst and with Tully's hand ever on her shoulder. The wet grass soaked her thin slippers and stockings. The night was so dark she could not see ten feet ahead of her. But the mountaineers walked as unerringly as though by broad daylight.

Not a word was spoken as they traversed the rich bottomland fields. In silence they filed across the narrow bridge that spanned the river with its myriad riffling rapids and shoals. They breasted the first steep trail leading upward into the heart of the Ramapos.

Then and then only did the five men abate their stealthy haste and dare to move with normal sound. Then and then only did Tully Bemis break silence.

"Your steady comp'ny's friend, Hardin, is like all the rest of them puddin'-heads down yonder," he informed the captive. "He locks nine doors and leaves the tenth door plumb open. He let you have that big collie purp of his'n to go to school and back with you, to scare off the Shivelys and them, and not a one of 'em would 'a' dared come anigh you after the way he beat up Roan. But he keeps the collie to home nights, instead of having it on the job over to Wallace's. If the dog had been to Wallace's to-night, he'd 'a' had to be croaked before he'd 'a' let us anywheres near the house. Wallace don't keep no dog. His wife don't like 'em. If more folks was afraid to keep dogs, there'd be easier pickings for them that makes their livings by what they can find in folks' housen at nights."

Sibyl did not heed his ruminative speech. But his breaking of the long silence emboldened her to ask the question that had been burning on her lips ever since the strange midnight journey began.

"Why did you risk prison to-night to kidnap me?" she demanded.

"I didn't risk nothing at all," he assured her.

"But when I am missed they will search the mountains from end to end," she went on. "Surely you must know that."

"Sure they will," he assented. "If they figger you went there. But they won't find you. Revnoo men and such-like cattle has searched these mountains for the last hundred years, off and on. And they didn't ever yet find anything we reely wanted to keep hid from them. There's lots of places in these mountains that nobody from outside can git to unless they're guided there. To-night you will be took where you're safe and comf'table. To-morrow night you'll be took where you're jest as safe, even if you ain't jest as comf'table. That is unless Bladen comes across before then. To-morrow night I aim to take you to my still. To-night it ain't fixed up nor provisioned. There wasn't time. So to-night I——"

"What has Mr. Bladen to do with it?" she broke in, astounded at Tully's confident mention of the geologist.

"He's got ev'rything to do with it," returned Bemis. "I'm holding you up here till he tells me where he found the treasure. If he don't tell me he don't ever get you back; and he don't ever get the treasure, either, because he's due to get shot from behind a rock first time he sets foot up here. I told him so."

"Told him so?" she echoed, her brain awhirl. "When?"

"I written him a letter," said Tully, "and I pinned it on Wallace's front door to-night when we come down there. Wallace is due to find it fust thing in the morning. He'll take it over to Bladen. I couldn't leave it to Hardin's on account of the dog being on watch there nights. But he'll get it safe enough. I didn't sign no name to it," he continued, in bland self-approval. "He won't know who written it. But I told him to write out just where the treasure is hid, and leave the writing on a rock he's been chipping at, up past Bear Swamp; and if the treasure is where he says, I'll send you back to Wallace's just as quick as I c'n clean out all of it and make a clean getaway. So that's———"

"Treasure?" she interrupted, more and more bemused by his boastful announcement. "What on earth are you talking about? If you mean that silly old legend about the Hessian treasure, then let me tell you Mr. Bladen has no more idea where it is than Arden Page has. He———"

"Sure he hain't!" agreed Tully, in elephantine sarcasm. "Certain sure he hain't! I know that. He hain't an idee where it is! That's what made him bawl out to you about finding it, this afternoon. That's why he showed you a handful of gold money from it, after him and you got through hugging one the other. I was there. I seen what I seen and likewise I hearn what I hearn. I——"

"*Oh!*" she broke in, enlightenment and disgust dawning together upon her perception. "You mean you were spying on us when I met Mr. Bladen this afternoon, on the way back from school? You were there when he caught me as I was falling and——"

"I was right there!" grinned Tully, guiding her deftly around an upward crook of the trail which was invisible to her night-dimmed eyes. "I was there, ma'am. But anyone in a mile could 'a' hearn him beller to you about how he'd found the treasure. He kep' a-hollering 'Gold! *Gold!* GOLD!' till it's a mericle they didn't hear him clear down to Pat'son. I——"

"But if you kept on listening," she urged, checking a hysterical desire to laugh at this weird conception of Bladen's exultation—"if you kept on listening, you must have heard him explain what he meant by the 'treasure' and by 'gold.' You must have heard him say it was——"

"I hearn all I had any call to hear. I hearn all I needed to hear," he declared. "I would 'a' got the secret out of him right then if it wouldn't of been for the dog. I didn't wait to hear any more. I hadn't any need to. It was time for me to get busy making him tell me where it was. Likewise he'll do it, unless he likes the money better than what he likes you. From the way he grabbed you, I guess you're the only thing he'd rather have than the treasure. That's why I'm giving him a chance to swap. He's due to——"

"But you're absolutely wrong!" she cried, in despair at his fatuous thick-headedness. "Can't you understand? Mr. Bladen is a scientist. He discovered a mineral deposit to-day

[140]

with tiny flecks of gold in it. To you or to me that would mean nothing. To a geologist it seemed a wonderful discovery. He was excited over it. To him it was real treasure-trove. Its cash value is nothing. He wasn't referring to that miserable Hessian treasure at all. Can't you see?"

"Yep," replied Tully, a note of real admiration in his thick voice. "Yep, I see; I see fine. I see he's got a girl that ain't afeard to lie something grand to help him out and to get herself free. It's a grand yarn, ma'am, but it leaks."

Chuckling, he relapsed into silence. Sibyl, her heart sinking, realized the utter futility of trying to make him believe.

The cat struggled and snarled as an especially rough bit of path joggled her. Sibyl risked a wholesale scratching of the hands by tightening her grasp on the spitting and twisting creature.

And so, for another half hour or more, they moved on in silence, over ridge and gully, ever deep and deeper into the mountains.

At last they came out on a razor-backed ridge above a cup-like depression wherein twinkled a cheerless light. Guiding her along the precipitous descent, Tully helped the girl down into the clearing in front of a squat log hut. The four Blue-eyed Niggers followed, running down the cliff-like slope with pantherine ease and sureness.

The twinkle of light from the window merged into a wider if not brighter radiance as the cabin door was opened. On the lighted threshold was silhouetted a bent little figure that gave no sign of greeting as Tully propelled his captive past her into the shack. He called back an indistinguishable dialect sentence over his shoulder at the four Blue-eyed Niggers, then closed the door on them.

"Those fellers are going to stick on watch outside all night, ma'am," he told Sibyl. "They ain't what you'd call pets, speshly when they know what they'll git if they let you go. So I wouldn't try to sneak past 'em if I was you."

Sibyl scarcely heard. Wide-eyed, she was taking in her squalid surroundings. The room wherein she stood was meagerly furnished. A primitive pallet against one wall served as a bed. Against the opposite wall was the battered cookstove. A rickety deal table with deep-dented surface held the kerosene lamp and one or two odds and ends. In a corner was an antique rocking-chair in last stages of uselessness. The only other place to sit down was a cracked and dirty old packing-box which stood close to the table and served as the sole dining-room chair.

The little crooked figure Sibyl had seen in the doorway now resolved itself into an unbelievably old and withered woman, with a face like wrinkled mahogany leather. Sibyl had seen her only once before. But Auntie Groot's face was not one to forget.

The old woman was eyeing her with bleary malevolence. In her hand was a flat bottle partly filled with a pale yellow fluid. From this she had very evidently been drinking, if one might judge by her expression and by the reek of raw new whisky on the close air of the room.

"It is good stuff, child," said Auntie Groot, ignoring the girl and addressing Bemis, while she waved the bottle explanatorily at him. "It is the best you have made. *Ak bedank ye.*"

"Here's another for you," responded Tully, exhuming a second bottle of moonshine from his pocket. "And I'll make good on the keg of it I said I'd give you for helping me out. It'll be here to-morrow night. Twenty-five gallon. Just like the stuff you've got there."

"It's worth more than twenty-five gallons—the *bodders en troble* this *meisje* will cause me," grumbled the old woman, her deep potations lifting to the surface a more plentiful number of ancient north Jersey Dutch phrases than usual. "And remember—if this brings the *wat* [law] up into thesen mountains, you take oath I shall not suffer by it?"

"Don't worry," exhorted Bemis. "She don't know who you are and she don't know where she is. Besides, you got ways to make her swear she won't ever squeal on you. Those fool folks down yonder in the valley don't break a word they've swore to. She'll keep an oath. Sleep quiet over that. I'll be back at dusk to-morrow to take her to the still, if her feller hain't made good by then. G' night."

He was gone, leaving Sibyl and the crone together in the hidden cabin. Paying no further heed to her guest, Auntie Groot walked somewhat waveringly over to the rocking-chair and sank down into its disreputable depths. There, rocking creakily to and fro, she applied herself repeatedly to the moonshine bottle, quaffing deeply and without softening the raw spirits with water.

Whisky was her one remaining delight in life, the one joy that never had palled. For a quart of it she would at any time have bartered what was left of her soul. Nothing short of the promise of a whole keg of the yearned-for stuff would have induced her to accede to Tully's request that she harbor his prisoner for a day and a night.

Fond as she was of Bemis, the bribe and a preliminary bottle of his moonshine had been needed to wheedle her into doing this risky thing for him.

[143]

Sibyl, still clasping the morose cat, seated herself on the packing-box at the table. Fascinated, sickened, she watched her hostess rock drunkenly to and fro and from time to time lift the flask to her withered lips. The sight was nauseating to the fastidious girl, yet it held in it an element of hope. If only the drinker should be overcome by her potations——

Presently, under the mellowing influence of high-proof new whisky, Auntie Groot was moved to song. In a reedy and hiccoughing ghost of a voice she droned forth the olden Jersey Dutch chant:

> *"De kutse'z an ed klaver*
> *De pertse'z an de haver*
> *De entse's an de waterplas—"*

The song slurred off into a mumble. Auntie Groot sat up very straight, glowering about her. Then she drank deeper from the flask, emptying it. After which she tried to rise, and could not; so, philosophically, she fell asleep.

Sibyl coughed loudly. The sleeper merely shifted her position in the depths of the old rocker and slept on.

The girl set down the cat, which started promptly on a discontented tour of the room, sniffing at everything and seeking vainly for some means of escape. Sibyl drew from her belt the pencil and the sheet of examination paper which she had thrust there when she saw Cleppy Bemis's face at the window of the Wallace living-room. She glanced again at the sleeper. Then she spread wide Dode Wyble's history paper and began feverishly to write on its unused side.

[144]

Fast she wrote, and concisely. When she had finished she took off the light gold bracelet—a Christmas gift from her father—which she wore on her left wrist. Pulling out two or three of her own long hairs, she wrapped the twisted note dexterously to the bangle with them, binding the paper close against the sides of the golden hoop.

Removing her shoes, she tiptoed across to where the cat crouched surlily beside the door. Holding the unwilling beast with one hand, she slipped the bracelet over Fluffy's head with some slight difficulty.

Thus the hoop of gold became a necklace for one of the ugliest old cats in northern New Jersey. Far from feeling honored by the adornment, Fluffy spat right venomously at her benefactress, and clawed in vain to remove the bracelet.

But Sibyl gave her no time for reflection. Unfastening the cabin's creaky door, she opened it a few inches.

On the instant, one of the Blue-eyed Niggers sprang up from the door-stone, to bar her way. As if chagrined that her attempt at escape had been thwarted, Sibyl closed the door again, without so much as disturbing Auntie Groot's slumbers.

During the second or two that she and the guard had spent in eyeing each other through the narrow strip of aperture, the cat had slipped out unobserved and had sped past the watcher, out into the darkness.

Back to the packing-box chair went Sibyl, and settled herself on it with a sigh of reaction.

"If it's true that cats have the homing instinct and always go straight back to where they live," she told herself, "some one at the Wallaces' may find my note and read it. If it isn't true—— Anyhow, it was the only chance!''

She shuddered a little, then braced herself against the creeping inroads of terror.

Sleepless, alert, she sat there on the cracked packing-box throughout the few remaining hours of darkness, while Auntie Groot snored noisily from the depths of the rocker.

At last the black oblong outside the window turned a murky gray. Then streaks of dawn light filtered in through it. One detail after another of the outer world became visible to the weary girl at the table. Trees took on form, stirring in the dawn wind. The sky waxed brighter and rosier.

Sibyl could see one of the four guards standing tirelessly in the middle of the clearing, slender and graceful as a Hindu boy, in his sodden rags. Behind him she could see a row of paintless beehives. From the nearest hive dangled a wisp of faded black cloth.

The sight reminded the girl of the symbol it depicted. In the hinterland of north Jersey many farmers still go to the hives, when a death has occurred in the family, and whisper mournfully to the bees, "So-and-so is dead!" Then a bit of crêpe is tied to one of the hives. It is an immemorial custom, brought over from Europe by the first settlers. This scrap of black cloth on Auntie Groot's hive had been there since the last death in her family, perhaps a quarter-century agone.

A black mongrel slouched across the clearing, on his way home to some Jackson White cabin after a night of forage. Sibyl's breath came fast. If such a dog—one of the throng that infest the mountains—should have encountered the cat during her way back to the valley——!

"I won't let myself think of it!" she declared, inwardly. "It's as easy to build air-castles as air-dungeons; and it is a million times pleasanter."

Auntie Groot stirred, muttered something incoherent in Jersey Dutch, then awoke.

CHAPTER

11

BRUCE HARDIN was miles deep in the ocean of slumber that engulfs an early-rising outdoor man most thoroughly an hour or two before he is due to awaken to the day's work. The May sun had not yet risen. The world was still gray and shimmering with the earliest dawn.

Hardin dreamed a right pleasant dream of winning every vegetable and live-stock prize at the Hohokus fair. The fair-grounds crowd was rapturous in its applause. Some one suggested that all the Hohokus bells be rung in the victor's honor. Instantly the bells were set a-peal. There were trillions of them and they all jangled deafeningly.

The crowd roared to Hardin for a speech. With Sibyl Gates at his side he arose to respond to the clamorous demand. He was resolved to make an inspired oration which should impress the girl he loved. But the multiple jangle of the bells drowned his words, filling all the universe with their metallic clash. In vexation, Bruce called to the ringers to be silent and let him make his speech.

The ringers did not obey, for the bells rang louder and more naggingly insistent than ever. But the jar of vexation roused Bruce from his dream, to confused wakefulness.

Though the dream had fled, the ringing kept on in the same maddeningly endless fashion. Gradually the sleep mists cleared from Hardin's senses. He realized that the telephone in the hall below was sending forth a furious clangor.

Grumbling, he got out of bed, cursing the idiot who presumably had gotten the wrong number and whose carelessness was robbing a sleepy man of his night's last and sweetest rest. Downstairs he padded, barefoot. He snatched the shiny black receiver from its shiny black hook and grunted an indignant query into the transmitter.

"That you, Bruce?" came Ethan Wallace's voice from the far end of the wire. "Good! After what we walked in on last night, Ma would have it that you and her had eloped. But I said she was crazy to talk like that. Just the same," a quaver of tense worry in the nasal voice, "she's gone! I called up because Ma said for me to make sure her and you——"

"What in blue blazes are you blithering about?" shouted Bruce, increasingly wrathful at being roused to listen to jargon which made no sense to him. "Are you trying to be funny or——?"

"I'm telling you Sibyl Gates is gone!" reiterated Wallace. "She's disappeared. Didn't take a thing with her, neither.

Didn't even change the clo'es she was wearing last evening. She's——"

"Gone?" croaked Hardin, an indefinable fear clutching at his heart. "What—what do you mean? She——"

"I mean what I say," answered Wallace, tartly. "Ma woke up ten minutes ago—woke up and smelled charring lamp wick all over the house. She figgered Sibyl had forgot to blow out the lamp when she got through with them examination papers. So she went downstairs to look. The lamp had burnt itself empty and the wick was all charred and smoking. So Ma went up to Sibyl's room, on the way to our room. The door was standing open and the bed hadn't been slept in. She woke me. She had a fool notion that you and teacher had maybe——"

"I'll be over there in five minutes!" interrupted Bruce, hoarse and disturbed.

He bounded up the stairs, and flung on his clothes in erratic haste, thrusting his bare feet into the boots that stood beside his bed. Coatless and collarless, he ran across lots at top speed to the Wallace homestead.

Mars, lying on the porch, leaped up and frisked gayly toward his master. But for once Bruce Hardin had neither word nor look for this collie chum of his. The dog galloped along at his side as Bruce dashed into the Wallace dooryard.

Wallace had seen him coming. He emerged from the house in shirt and trousers, and barefooted. Behind him, in the doorway, stood his wrappered and curl-papered wife, her fat face creased with worry.

"What in Sam Hill do you make of it, Bruce?" demanded Wallace as his neighbor came within earshot. "It ain't a mite like Sibyl to sneak off, without a word, leaving the lamp burning. It might 'a' exploded and everything! She——"

"And," tremblingly proclaimed Mrs. Wallace from the doorway, "she never took a stitch of extra clothing along with her, nor even her satchel. And she didn't even take her pocketbook. It's right in her top drawer, with all the money still in it. It don't make sense."

"No note, neither," chimed in Wallace. "Just vanished-like. It——"

"Oh dear!" moaned his wife. "I do wish things wouldn't happen out of turn. It does upset a body so! There's poor precious Fluffy! She's gone, too. This is the first morning in ten whole years or more that Fluffy hasn't come running up to me, so cunning-like, for her saucer of milk, the minute I open the door. She——"

"Perhaps Miss Gates's disappearance is a trifle more important than the cat's," testily suggested Bruce, his temper fraying at Mrs. Wallace's coupling of his sweetheart's absence with that of the miserable feline. "You're sure she is nowhere in the house? Nor——?"

"Nowheres at all," insisted Mrs. Wallace. "Not a sign of her anywheres. I wouldn't 'a' believed—— Oh, good!" she broke off, her voice scaling half an octave through delight. "There's Fluffy, anyhow! Fluffy's come home to us, even if Sibyl hasn't!"

Choking back a hot retort, Bruce followed the direction of the good woman's beaming gaze. From the direction of the river the unbeautiful Fluffy was strolling morosely into the dooryard. She limped, and she was more than wontedly bedraggled and woebegone.

Mrs. Wallace waddled forward to greet her pet and to welcome the scrawny beast home. But before she could reach the returned prodigal Mars created a diversion on his own account.

The collie had been lying quietly at his master's feet, looking up with troubled eyes into Bruce's harassed face, as though sensing the man's nervous worry. Now, at sight of Fluffy, the dog rushed at the cat like a furry whirlwind, his deep-set dark eyes dancing with gay mischief.

Mrs. Wallace cried out in alarm. Bruce was about to order the dog back to his side, when a perverse imp within his brain prevented him from interfering. Mrs. Wallace had rejoiced so mightily in the cat's return, and had displayed so much less emotion over Sibyl's absence, that he hoped morbidly his collie would catch the forlorn animal and rip her to ribbons.

Fluffy, however, was not minded to be slain in her own dooryard after her long night's wanderings. With a yowl she skittered up an apple tree, from whose lowest bough she caterwauled and spat defiance at the racketing and leaping dog below.

"Come back here, Mars," Hardin commanded, belatedly and in no great fervor.

Reluctantly the dog obeyed, trotting back to his master with a penitent air which was belied by the merry glint in his eye and the quiver of his little tulip ears.

"Kitty, kitty, kitty!" wheedled Mrs. Wallace, from beneath the bough. "Come on down to me, like a good little cat. That wicked dog shan't hurt you. He—— Land's sakes!" she shrilled, in the midst of her honeyed exhortations, "if Fluffy hasn't got a gold collar around her sweet throat! Look, Eth! Fluffy's got a gold collar! Where in this wide world did she get such a thing?"

Bruce eyed the phenomenon with no special interest. There in the strengthening light crouched the cat in the bough fork. Around her scant-haired neck dangled a circlet which shone bright in the dawn glow.

Then all at once Hardin's glance narrowed. Twisted around part of the bracelet was a soakingly wet and very dirty screw of paper. He took a step forward.

"That's no collar," Ethan Wallace was saying in gaping amaze. "That's teacher's gold bracelet. I'd know the funny filigree work on it anywheres. It's——"

He got no further. With a bound Bruce Hardin had reached the tree. Lithely he swung himself up to the bough and seized the spitting and wiggling cat by the neck.

With none too tender fingers Hardin tugged the golden bracelet off the neck of the squirming and miauing Fluffy, getting the back of his hand lavishly scratched for his pains.

Then he lowered himself to earth and began to unwind the strands of bright hair from around the thin-twisted paper which encircled half the bracelet. Fluffy, released, fled spitting to the house and vanished under the kitchen porch; the gleesomely pursuing Mars reaching that refuge a bare sixteenth of a second behind her.

Bruce's strong fingers fumbled as he unfastened the hair and opened the wet and bedraggled sheet of paper. Holding it to the light, he read the inspired words of Dode Wyble on the theme of our country's discovery:

"It is diskvred in 8een92 by Cuolmbs but uncle Tice ses thats a dam lie it is diskvred by Gorge Wasngton a cuple of yeers or moar befoar then and——"

[153]

"It's that idiotic examination paper she was correcting last evening!" exclaimed Bruce, in bewilderment. "But why should it be fastened to her bracelet around your cat's throat, when——?"

He ceased his idle conjecture. As he spoke he had turned the smudgy sheet over. On its reverse side were penciled lines in Sibyl Gates's strong handwriting. These he scanned aloud, muttering their words so fast in his excitement that the Wallaces were barely able to catch his meaning.

"I am a prisoner in Auntie Groot's cabin," he read. "Cleppy Bemis knocked on the window as I was working over the examination papers, and beckoned to me. I went out on the porch. Two men caught hold of me and gagged and held me. They were Blue-eyed Niggers and they and two more with them were under the orders of Tully Bemis. I promised Bemis I'd come along quietly (he was going to knock me senseless and carry me if I didn't) if he would let me bring Fluffy along.

"I am fastening this note to her neck. (God grant it is true that cats make straight for home as soon as they are let out of a strange place!) Bemis brought me here for to-night. To-morrow he is going to come back and hide me more safely in his still, he says, 'where nobody can find me.' He says he will keep me a prisoner till Horace Bladen tells him where the Hessian treasure is hidden. I told him Mr. Bladen didn't know anything about the treasure or even if it exists. But of course he didn't believe me. He says I will never be allowed to come home unless Mr. Bladen tells him where the treasure is.

"If any of you know how to find Auntie Groot's cabin, won't you come and get me out before it's too late? But several of you must come together, and armed. Four of the Blue-eyed Niggers are guarding the cabin, and Tully Bemis would be able to rouse all the Jackson Whites. Don't worry too much about me. I am all safe—thus far. SIBYL GATES."

As Bruce finished his dazed perusal a babel of incoherent exclamations burst from Ethan Wallace and his wife. Hardin stilled them with a fierce gesture.

"Shut up!" he shouted. "And listen to me. Wallace, go to the phone and get hold of the nearest police and Bladen and as many other men as you can round up in a rush. Don't waste time. It'll be better to start in time enough with too few men, than start too late with enough of them. Hustle! Go to Tully Bemis's shack. You know where it is. If I'm not there, go on to Auntie Groot's. I'm going to interview Bemis, first of all. He is the soul of the whole thing. Without him, none of the others will raise a hand to keep her from us."

Hardin called back the last few words over his shoulder as he turned and ran across the field toward the river.

"The crazy fool!" wailed Ethan Wallace, starting for the telephone. "He's gone up there without so much as a stick to defend himself with. By this time the mountains will be buzzing. If he ain't shot from ambush, Tully Bemis'll kill him. Everyone'll know what he's there for. He——"

The perturbed farmer finished his lament by ringing vigorously the telephone bell. His wife, more practical in an emergency, sent up a shrill screech for the hired man. Then she went indoors and loaded her husband's ancient shotgun, in preparation for his punitive excursion in the Ramapos.

[155]

Wallace had erred in saying Bruce was going into the mountains unarmed. Alongside the running man frisked Mars, his great red-gold collie—almost as stanch a helper, in a tight corner, as any gun could have been. Sensing his master's wild excitement, the collie galloped at full speed ahead of him and around him, gayly eager for whatsoever adventure might befall.

Reaching the foot of the mountains, Bruce slackened his pace to a mile-eating stride as he climbed the first steep acclivity. He knew he might well have reason to expect violent action before he should descend that trail again, and he was not minded to wear down his glorious athletic strength prematurely. There might be stark need for all of it he could summon to his aid before the morning's happenings should be at an end.

In his brain the first swirlingly murderous rage against Bemis was settling into an ice-cold deadly fury. He could picture the gallant defenseless girl seized and carried off to the vile Groot cabin by him, the terror that must have underlain the calm note she tied to the bracelet. His heart turned to black bitterness within him at the thought of the treatment accorded her by the giant.

Through his wrath he was aware of a thrill of utter admiration for her cool resourcefulness in taking Fluffy along to serve as unconscious bearer of her message to her friends. The trick was so simple, and yet it had been ingenious enough to fool a man like Bemis!

Into Hardin's love for the girl was now woven veneration for her pluck and her wit. He rejoiced that he and he alone should be hastening to her rescue and to the punishment of the brute beast who had kidnapped and threatened her.

With the wave of exultant love came a tenfold intensifying of the hate he bore Tully Bemis for what he had done. A berserk battle lust flared up within him at the prospect of coming to grips with the giant.

He felt he had been right in his hurried decision to go straight to Bemis's cabin, before journeying to Auntie Groot's.

"To-morrow he is going to come back," a phrase in the note had said. That must mean that Tully had taken her to Auntie Groot's and had left her there, returning presumably to his own cabin.

The chances were that Bemis would still be at home, in this pre-sunrise hour, after having been abroad so late the night before.

Yes, it was wisest to go direct to him before continuing the journey to where the girl was hidden. With Bemis dead or captured, the timorous Jackson Whites would not dare face the consequences of his lawless act. The return with Sibyl would be easy.

On the other hand, should he go at once to Auntie Groot's cabin, even could he break past the four guards Sibyl had written of, word of it would travel with the speed of light to Tully. The giant and a score of his armed fellow-mountaineers would be certain to intercept the return trip. No, Tully must be dealt with first, and dealt with in such way as to put him definitely out of the contest.

The possibility that others of the Jackson Whites might be with him at his cabin, as potential reinforcements, did not trouble Bruce. The illogical battle-craving was singing in his brain. The more foes the merrier.

As he sped on upward he found himself wondering

amazedly at Tully's daring in kidnapping a woman from her boarding-place and keeping her a captive in the mountains. Bemis must have known that such a crime assuredly would bring him foul of the law.

The law and the public at large have scant sympathy for a kidnapper or abductor. This Jackson White criminal was no fool. He must have known he was inviting a many-year term in prison. The average mountaineer has an almost superstitious terror of jail.

Yet Bemis had done this unbelievable thing with no other professed motive—according to Sibyl's note—than to hold her for ransom until Bladen should tell him where the Hessian treasure was hidden! Blinking Horace Bladen, of all men! As though Horace could know anything about the mythical whereabouts of the mythical treasure! Oh, the mountaineer must be insane!

Yet, Bruce's memory of Tully Bemis was not of a maniac. Daft he might be on the subject of the treasure, from long brooding. But he was not the man to steal and hold a girl for ransom on a mere unfounded notion that one of her friends might perhaps have a clue to the hoard's cache. It did not make sense.

Nor did Bruce's overfull mind dwell long on this unprofitable theme. He could hold no consecutive thought, in that hour of supreme rage and supreme love, except for the dire punishment of the man who had stolen Sibyl.

CHAPTER

12

TULLY BEMIS had gone to bed as soon as he returned from leaving Sibyl at Auntie Groot's. He had slept as sweetly and refreshingly as any child. Indeed, so well did he slumber that he did not wake until the triple challenge-bark of his black mongrel hounds aroused him.

Then he sat up in bed to find the sun was rising and that his three dogs were shattering the sunrise silences of the mountain-tops with their wild clangor.

As Tully knew, and as every dog man knows, there are as many cadences and meanings to a dog's various kinds of barks as to the tones of human speech. Were some mountain neighbor strolling along the trail at this early hour, the three black curs might well have announced the newcomer's presence by a casual bark or two. Had they been startled by some unexpected sound or sight, they might have given tongue with the mild excitement of curiosity.

But their barks now were savagely truculent. They were barks of hot defiance to an outlander enemy. There was no mistaking the timbre of their racket.

Tully Bemis jumped out of bed—he had gone to sleep, as usual, in shirt and trousers, merely kicking off his boots and removing his vest—and crossed to the door, whence he could command a view of the trail from below and from above.

At the far edge of his sloping dooryard his black hounds were capering about, hackles abristle, heading toward a bend in the trail a hundred feet beneath and making the air resound with their challenge-barks. Sound and scent had told them, seconds earlier, of an intruder's approach.

Tully Bemis took in the scene, his own gaze focusing on the turn in the trail below the cabin. Not once in five years did any save a Jackson White ascend that trail at so early an hour of the day.

Then around the bend came bounding a huge red-gold collie. Close at his heels hastened a man. Bemis recognized both. His keen vision gave him a momentary glimpse of Bruce Hardin's set face.

Not for an instant did the mountaineer misunderstand the meaning of this sunrise visit. Hardin was not searching vaguely for the lost girl, as might one who had heard merely that she had disappeared and who came to look in the mountains for her. No, there was swift purpose in his every stride and in every line of his tense body.

His face was white and murderous, and he was making

straight for Tully Bemis's cabin. There could be no doubt
as to his intentions, no hope that perhaps he did not know
Bemis's part in the kidnapping.

Intuitive as a wild animal, the mountaineer saw and
understood. This was not a time to stand and parley and to
pretend wondering innocence. Hardin had come to act,
not to talk. Tully knew that, without stopping to analyze
how he knew it.

The truth flashed on him in the fraction of a second during which he first caught a glimpse of the ascending man
and collie. Later there might be time to wonder why and
how Hardin could possibly have learned so early of Sibyl's
abduction and Bemis's responsibility for it. Just now there
was mortal need for action. To judge from Bruce's face,
it was a case of kill or be killed.

Through Bemis's new-wakened senses surged a rage as
homicidal as Bruce's own. By learning of the abduction
this outlander farmer had set Tully's golden plans at
naught. Unless he could be gotten rid of, then good-by to
Bemis's hopes of forcing Bladen to tell where the Hessian
hoard was hidden! Good-by to his life ambitions and to his
glowing dreams of fortune!

There was nothing for it but to rid himself of Hardin
and to trust that none other of the valley folk had discovered
his share in Sibyl's kidnapping. Bemis had been playing
too daringly and for too high stakes to permit himself to
lose his lifetime's prize while he had strength and cunning
to fight for it.

His swart face flaming, his brain afire, Bemis went into
action.

Pointing to the oncoming man and collie who had barely

rounded the curve of the trail below him, Tully yelled to his dogs:

"Git 'em, boys! *S-s-sic!*"

The three black brutes needed no more than their master's bare permission—to say nothing of his eager encouragement—to send them tearing ferociously down the slope to wreak slaughter on the invaders. Naturally savage as tigers, only Bemis's sharp training had prevented them, all their lives, from assailing every stranger—man or beast—they chanced to encounter among the hills. Not relishing the thought of a fine or of a court order to kill his dogs, Tully had ever held them in check, except when wreaking punishment on some luckless Jackson White who had offended him.

Now with voice and gesture he loosed them in all their fury on the two trespassers who were coming to threaten his life aspirations. Like flung spears the three gaunt black brutes bore down upon their victims.

At sound of Tully's voice Bruce Hardin had looked up. For the merest flash of time the two men's fierce eyes met. Then, breaking into a charging run, Bruce swarmed up the slope toward his enemy. Heedless of the oncoming triple black avalanche he sped, Mars at his side.

Tully did not await his foe's coming. He stepped back into the house, barring its stout door and flinging wide the high and small window alongside it.

If Bruce had had scope for caution or even for common sense he would have read aright the sinister meaning of this double move. But his heart was aflame with the yearning to get at the kidnapper of the girl he loved. On he came.

Then he was cognizant of the three black devils that

swept down the slope at him. Mars, growling, spun forward to meet them and to break their charge before it could crash into his master.

Without checking his run, Bruce whipped a handkerchief from his shirt pocket, at the same time ordering Mars behind him. He recalled, in the heat of the moment, an old trick described to him by a hired man of his father's, years before—a man who had uncanny knowledge of the ways and the thinking processes of dogs.

As the foremost and largest of the three dogs tore at him, Bruce came to a momentary halt, bracing himself as of old on the football field. At the same time he caught two opposite corners of the white handkerchief and held it stretched taut, well in front of him.

The onrushing black dog leaped for him, its foaming jaws instinctively snapping at that bar of white cloth held so invitingly between it and its prey. As the black mongrel leaped, the braced athlete kicked.

The toe of his thick boot smote the dog with appalling force in mid-abdomen. It was such a kick as had more than once scored a goal for Hardin's eleven in college days. It carried the skilled dynamic power of a mule's kick as it smashed into its mark.

With a gasping howl the big black dog collapsed, writhing and foaming, on the rocky hillside. Fight and strength and power of locomotion were gone. Of the three formidable Bemis dogs—the terrors of the mountain region—only two remained.

"Mars!" sung out Hardin, breaking into a run once more; then as the collie came whirling forward: "*Take* 'em, Mars! You ought to be able to handle both of them."

[163]

The collie needed no second bidding. The two remaining dogs were flying at him. Straight at them he dashed. They parted as Mars closed in, meaning, after the manner of their kind, to fall upon him from either side.

But Mars belonged to the breed into whose tulip ears the ghosts of warring wolf ancestors whisper their olden battle secrets in moments of stress. He did not wait to be borne down by a cur on either hip. Wheeling to the left, in mid-charge, he flung himself on one of the dogs before it could whirl to face him.

One slash of his saber-like white eyetooth and he had slit the black hide from shoulder to loin. The wounded mongrel tore at him; so did its comrade. Leaping backward, Mars eluded the double rush, diving under the high-bounding body of the unhurt cur, and, as he went, slashing deep into the shaggy black stomach.

The first dog dived for the collie's slim foreleg, to break it. But the leg was not there when the grinding jaws clashed at it. And the cur found itself the worse for a nip on the side of the head that ripped off half an ear.

There was no more time for footwork and skirmishing, for the second dog had taken advantage of this moment of maneuvering to throw himself bodily on the collie. Down went the three in an unloving triple embrace, snarling, snapping, rending, screaming. Together thus they rolled down the steepest part of the slope, the collie keeping his legs tucked under him and his compact body pressed into a furry ball, his flying jaws industriously at work on both adversaries in a series of whirlwind bites and slashes. It was a glorious scrimmage. Mars was having the time of his life. Always, in his fastidious thoroughbred soul, he had detested the hulking black curs of the mountains. Never before had he had what he considered a fair chance to wreak that hate. That the battle might well end in his own death did not mar in any way his joy in it.

Heedless of the roaring dog fight behind him, Bruce Hardin stormed up the few intervening yards between himself and the newly shut door of the Bemis cabin. For an instant the distorted face of Tully appeared at the high little window. He was grasping something metallic and rusty.

Then came a ripping explosion as he fired almost point blank at the advancing Hardin.

Bruce noted subconsciously the advent of the leveled gun and he threw himself on his hands and knees as Tully pulled trigger. The unexpectedness and speed of the action disconcerted Bemis's snap aim. The charge of duck-shot roared above the farmer, one pellet plowing a flesh graze along his back.

Bruce was up on the instant, plunging forward and snatching at the protruding gun barrels. Before he was fairly upon his feet, before Bemis could guess what he was doing or could tighten his own casual hold on stock and trigger or could fire again, Hardin had seized the rusty muzzle of the gun and had heaved with all his strength, holding the muzzle aside from his own chest.

Not looking for such a seemingly insane move, Tully had not been holding the gun with more than ordinary firmness. The lightning-quick wrench tore it from his grasp even as he pulled trigger for the second time.

The shot went wild, but the recoil drove the fore sight into Bruce's fingers, cutting them almost to the bone.

Still brandishing the empty gun by the muzzle, Hardin threw himself at the ancient door of the cabin. The window, he knew, was too small for him to climb through, even if such a move would not have put him at the mercy of the man inside.

The gun butt clanged against the upper panel of the door. The oak split from top to bottom. A second crash of the walnut butt and three more cracks gaped into view, while the door groaned as if in pain, at the fury of the assault.

The third blow knocked the panel in. But it also splintered the strong gun butt, leaving only the twisted double barrel in Bruce's bleeding hands.

Athwart the gaping hole in the door stuck the bar that held it shut. Without waiting to get his breath after the swift hail of blows on the panel, Bruce struck once more, this time upward, his gun barrels knocking the bar out of its groove and sending it rattling to the room floor just as Bemis recovered from his daze of surprise and sprang to fasten it in place.

Failing, Tully put his giant shoulder to the broken door, to hold it shut against the incomer, while he tugged his broad-bladed claspknife out of his pocket and yanked it open.

He was a fraction of a second too late in applying his tremendous strength to the broken portal. For, before he could get leverage or brace himself, Bruce Hardin had lifted the latch and had slammed his own body with all his strength against the oak. Under that onset the door gave, not far, but far enough. Instantly Tully was braced to shut it and hold it shut. But he was too late.

[166]

With snakelike swiftness, Bruce slipped in through the momentarily open space, barely escaping being caught between door and jamb as Bemis's weight crashed belatedly against the shivered paneling.

As his enemy burst in, Bemis wheeled on him, lunging for his throat with the claspknife. The stroke was delivered with the driving urge of an engine piston, and with a practiced speed that would have driven it blade-deep had it found its mark.

But even as he slid into the room Bruce anticipated some attack on the part of his unwilling host, by dodging back out of reach of whatsoever blow should fall. At sight of the blade's flash he changed his dodge to a backward spring, to avoid it.

The shearing blade missed its mark by a matter of inches. Before it could strike again, Hardin had leaped back six feet from it, snatching at a stool for the recovery of his balance. Bemis hurled his heavy knife at the stumbling Bruce's throat.

Like many another Ramapo mountaineer, Tully possessed rare prowess in this art of knife-throwing. A hundred times, for fun, he and his fellows had practiced it—had practiced it until some of them could be certain that when the weapon should find its target it would strike, point forward, and with enough momentum to cleave a half-inch plank.

Supreme was Bemis among local knife-throwers, as in strength and brain and gameness. Now he hurled with all his wild energy and skill, aiming for the throat of his antagonist.

The knife whizzed through the room like a giant bee.

More by instinct than by reason, as he saw the other's hurling gesture, Bruce flung up one arm to ward it off. It was the arm whose hand had grasped the stool.

Up went the arm and up went the oaken stool. Deep into the stool's battered seat the blade penetrated and stood quivering.

By the time it had reached its unintended goal Bruce Hardin dropped the stool and sprang barehanded at Tully.

Bemis met him more than halfway, their mighty bodies coming together with an impact that jarred the solid old cabin to its shallow foundations.

As his foe charged, Bruce set himself and sent his left fist with full force at the unshaven jaw. It was a blow delivered hard enough to knock out the average professional pugilist. But it did not land.

Somewhere during his days at reform school or in prison or during his period of hiding in the slums of Paterson, Tully Bemis had picked up rudiments of boxing. Not abating his own rush, he shifted his head to one side. Bruce's fist flashed past his jaw, merely scoring the side of the giant's face.

It was then that they came together with a breath-taking shock and grappled chest to chest.

From time immemorial mountaineers have wrestled, in preference to boxing. It is their chosen sport. Bemis had thrown with ease every mountain wrestler from Suffern to Pompton. Moreover, there was no dirty trick of close-quarters rough-and-tumble fighting of which he was not master.

Yet in the shorter and slighter farmer he was meeting his toughest opponent. Years of football as well as of mat

[168]

work in the college gym had given Bruce a wrestling style
of his own. Foot to foot, knee to knee, breast to breast, he
met his formidable adversary.

Back and forth swayed and stamped and heaved the
two, their breath coming in grunts, their feet hammering
the floor for balance and for leverage. The ancient rickety
table, the big stove, and the rest of the meager furniture
were upset and smashed by their reeling bodies and stamping feet. Ten-year-old dust arose in choking clouds around
them. Dust caught in spider webs among the rafters came
snowing down upon them.

Trick after trick, force after force, one and the other put
forth, only to be blocked. Twice Hardin averted by a hair's-
breadth a gouge for the eyes from Tully's pronged fingers.
Once he shrank aside barely far enough to avoid an upward
jerk of Bemis's knee-cap into his groin. The giant was making use of every mountain barroom maneuver as well as
such legitimate moves of the game as he had mastered.

As Tully shifted for an underhold, Bruce tore free, leaving part of his shirt in the larger man's grasp. As he broke
loose he struck, sending an uppercut to the giant's jaw. It
grazed Bemis's chin, but landed flush on his nose, from below, breaking it.

At once Bruce was at the mountaineer with a shower of
short-arm blows, keeping free of the other's terrible arm-
grip and forcing him to box.

This, for a minute, Tully was avidly willing to do, but
almost at once he saw his mistake. If Bruce had erred at
the outset by underestimating Bemis's possible knowledge
of boxing, it became quickly apparent now that as a boxer
the Jackson White was in no way Hardin's match.

[169]

Blow after blow Bruce rained in upon the face and the wind and the heart of the giant, blows delivered with a deadly precision and with whale-bone snap and punishing power. Bemis guarded as best he could, but he was hopelessly outmatched.

Seeing this, and in torment from his merciless drubbing, he sought with all his might and with all his wile to come to grips again. But Hardin would not have it so. Lightly he backed away from Tully's all-encompassing arm-sweeps, designed to draw him into their terrible clutch. When he was forced to clinch, he did so in such way as to break loose at will.

Not once did he allow Bemis's arms to gather him in. And all the time he was slugging with every atom of scientific prowess, seeking out vulnerable spots and belaboring them with smashes that set the giant reeling and coughing.

There could be but one logical end to such fearful bombardment, with such trained strength behind it. Unhurt, tireless, Bruce fought on, here and there and everywhere at once, side-stepping or ducking or blocking most of Tully's increasingly slow efforts to retaliate with swings and lunges of the hamlike fists which had spread fear throughout the Ramapos.

Hardin was landing almost at will. Every blow was shaking Tully to the very core of his being. Bruce fought with a deadly and icy calm. He had come hither for a purpose. He was fulfilling that purpose in hideously efficient manner.

He was merciless. The memory of Bemis's abominably foul tactics during their grapple, as well as the thought of Sibyl's treatment at his hands, had dried up Hardin's

[170]

springs of pity. He neither wished quarter nor intended to grant it.

From outside came the snarling din of the triple dog fight. In the room the slam of bare fist against bare flesh was like the tattoo of drums. The dust clouds swirled stiflingly around the battlers. They stumbled amid the wreckage of furniture.

With a wild rally, Bemis drove Bruce clean across the room before him, slugging and boring in. Hardin gave ground willingly before the heavier and larger man, sooner than be caught in his strangling grip. As he retreated he continued to avoid the other's smashes and to pour in counter-blows at every vulnerable point above the belt. Tully's own momentum lent added power to the punches which rained on him as he attacked.

At the far end of the room Bruce's right heel touched the wall, warning him he could retreat no further. He made as though to side-step out of the way. Bemis foresaw the sideward slip, and to prevent it he hurled himself bodily upon the slighter enemy.

As Tully did so, Hardin gave over his feint at slipping out of the way, braced himself, and sent a short-arm uppercut to the jaw. Bemis was hurtling forward when the unforeseen punch was delivered. His entire warped mentality was taken up in keeping Bruce from side-stepping from the wall against which the mountaineer's greater bulk and weight were pinning him. Thus he ran, full tilt, into Hardin's uppercut.

The shock of the impact lifted Bemis's bare feet clean from the floor an inch or two. His knees doubled limply under him and he tumbled, inert, on his face. It was a clean knockout.

Panting, dizzy, Bruce stepped backward, looking down at the giant he had overthrown. His arm tingled and throbbed from the concussion. His knuckles were raw. Two of his fingers were sprained. His clothes, above the waist, were torn off, as were Bemis's, and they hung in flapping streamers about his hips.

But he had conquered. His foe lay bruised and bleeding and senseless. Sibyl's kidnapping was in some part avenged. Sibyl's safe return was in some part assured. Now to bind the prisoner in such a way as to hold safe until the arrival of Wallace and the rest. In another quarter-hour at most they must reach the Bemis cabin. Then, Tully safely turned over to them, he could go to the release of Sibyl.

Hardin felt an odd elation, as might a victorious knight errant of old or a slayer of some dragon that had imprisoned a fairytale princess. Seldom in these drab twentieth-century days is it given to man to do physical battle for the woman he loves. The glow of it went to Bruce's head, like strong drink.

But there was no time to waste. His blow had stunned Bemis, yet its effects could be but momentary on so tough a constitution as the giant mountaineer's. Even now Tully was stirring and mumbling, a bare five seconds after his downfall. On a system such as his the knockout could leave but a brief effect. In another minute or so, at most, he would be himself again, once more as potentially dangerous as a rattlesnake.

A hank of stout set-line hung on a wall peg. Bruce crossed to it and took it down, testing its resistance by tugging at it here and there. It was as good as new. It would make an ideal binding for any man's arms and ankles. Uncoiling it, Hardin went back to where Tully still lay inert on his face.

The giant no longer twitched and muttered. He lay as moveless as though he were dead. Bruce was puzzled. In his boxing experience, a knocked-out man's recovery is swift and steady, after once he begins to mumble. Aparently he had struck even harder than he realized, that or else Bemis's powers of recuperation were unduly slow.

He bent down above Tully, cord in hand, to turn him over. Heaving doughtily, he began to shift Bemis's position so as to get at his wrists.

The giant was as flaccid and limp as a shot squirrel. Then, under his own hands, Bruce felt a sharp tensing of Tully's body. But he realized its meaning a second too late.

With the speed of a striking copperhead Tully wrenched himself sideways and caught the ankles of the unsuspecting man who leaned over him. In the same moment he tugged them toward him.

Bruce Hardin crashed to the floor, on his back, with an impetus that knocked the breath out of him and that rapped the back of his skull against the flooring with half-stunning shock.

By the time he touched ground Tully was atop him, kneeling agonizingly on his chest and stomach.

Bemis's mighty fingers—the fingers that could twist a horseshoe—found their death-hold in the prostrate Hardin's throat.

CHAPTER

13

COCKSURE of his hard-won victory and with his senses dulled by fatigue and strenuous exertion, Bruce had failed for once to take into account the inborn craftiness of the mountaineers.

He would not have taken a seemingly dead fox out of a trap without guarding against the wily beast's coming to life with a lacerating bite at its captor. Yet he had given Bemis a full half-minute to come back to his senses, and then had leaned unwarily over the shamming giant with both hands occupied in turning him over.

Even in the daze of the moment, as the tables were turned so dramatically upon the careless victor of the fight, Bruce Hardin felt a twinge of self-contempt at his own criminal negligence in allowing himself to be caught by so old and simple a ruse.

True, Bemis had been knocked unconscious. But he had been senseless for only a second or so at most, as Hardin realized now. The rest of the time he had played 'possum while co-ordination of muscle and clearness of thought came back to him and while he schemed to outmaneuver his conquerer.

Flat on his back lay Bruce Hardin, Tully's vast weight crushing him down, Tully's ragged knees digging into his chest and stomach, Tully's vise-grip on the throat choking the life out of him.

Above him flamed the bleeding and swollen face, its puffedly discolored eyes glaring red murder down into his own. There was no glint of mercy there, nor of fair play. There was nothing but homicide.

The digging fingers had found Bruce's jugular. They were cutting off breath and life together from the tortured farmer. Insane with rage and pain, Bemis was killing his foe in approved cave-man style, by throttling him.

Through the riot of pain and choking, Bruce's mind cleared from the jar of his skull's impact with the floor. As ever in times of stark peril, his thoughts shone with abnormal clearness. Not fictionally romantic thoughts of his past life or of his ended career or even of Sibyl, but thoughts of extricating himself from his seemingly inextricable dilemma.

With clear thought came instant action, just as it had done in some vital crisis in football.

Drawing his legs far up under him, and exerting his every atom of resilient muscle, he threw his upper body high and to one side. The jerk of the sudden motion—one of the best-known of myriad wrestling devices—jarred

[175]

THE FAITH OF A COLLIE

Bemis's knees off the flesh they were grinding into, and destroyed his precarious center of gravity.

From under him wriggled Hardin, eel-like in his slippery speed. But though he was free of the incubus that had been crushing his chest and wind, he had not rid himself of that viselike throathold. Even as the two men struggled side by side on the floor, Tully did not slacken that strangling grasp of his on the smaller man's throat—a hold which, in a few seconds more, at most, could not fail to achieve its lethal aim.

Pain and his cut-off breath added wild vehemence to Hardin's counter-assault. Bemis's hands were both busy with his throat. Thus Tully was unable to guard himself against such attack.

As he shifted from under the giant, Hardin made use of a trick taught him by his old boxing master—a renowned rough-and-tumble fighter in his day. Ordinarily, Bruce would have hesitated to do such a thing, though no rules of bare-hand fighting forbid it. But something effective must be done instantly if that murder pressure was to be loosed from his throat in time.

Bringing both clenched fists against Bemis's temples, Bruce gouged deep with the middle fingers' knuckles into the very center of each temple. With all his remaining power he did this. And it served its turn.

There are few more unendurable forms of anguish than this forcible boring of a strong man's knuckles into an adversary's temple hollows. It is a vitally vulnerable spot, where nerves are many and the skull bone is thin. No mortal can withstand that grinding pressure, scientifically applied.

Within five seconds Tully had loosed his grasp of Bruce's

throat to thrust aside from his own temples those torment-inflicting knuckles. He reared himself upward to attack again.

As Tully's fingers left Bruce's throat Hardin did two things simultaneously. He drew a huge breath into his tortured lungs. At the same time he leaped up and caught the half-risen Bemis by left wrist and right knee, bringing his own head and shoulders under the other's stomach.

It was a Herculean effort, for all his perfect leverage and it strained his every sinew—this dynamic up-starting, with the vast and struggling weight of Bemis above him. It well-nigh made Bruce collapse under it.

But to his feet he reeled, Tully still held above him by knee and wrist. The whole move did not occupy two seconds. It was too brief for Bemis to wrench free or to find a bracing spot for his own waving legs.

Reaching a semi-upright posture, Bruce in the same motion heaved Tully forward through space, in the ancient "spread-eagle" throw. He had turned his own body into a catapult, with Bemis as its projectile.

Forward through the air sailed the giant, arms and legs wide, victim of a Cornish wrestling trick that was old when his first ancestors came to America—a trick whose success depends wholly on surprise and on leverage.

Against the wall of the room, five feet away, he crashed, shoulder on.

To the floor he fell resoundingly, right arm and collarbone broken, left leg twisted helplessly under him, fractured at the ankle.

The fight was over.

Swaying drunkenly, half suffocated, in dire pain, his

muscles wrenched agonizingly by the spread-eagle exploit, Bruce Hardin collapsed on to an overturned chair and fought for breath.

No need now to keep on the alert, even if he had had the ability left to do so. There could be no doubting that the giant was crushed and helpless as he lay sprawling there. One is not spread-eagled against a hard wall by a human catapult without sustaining injuries which call for hospital care.

For perhaps two minutes Bruce sat, relaxed and gasping. Then the mists began to disperse from before his eyes and his breath came and went with less anguished labor. Still shaken and suffering he pulled himself together.

Bemis had ceased to moan, and lay watching him as might a broken-backed rattlesnake. The mountaineer was in dire pain, but his courage and coolness had come back to him. Judging Bruce by himself, he expected nothing short of death by torture so soon as Hardin should have recovered breath and motion. Yet fearlessly he lay waiting his doom.

Hardin arose and came toward the stricken giant, standing over him and looking down. Unflinchingly Tully glowered back at him. His body was conquered; his spirit was not. Bruce nodded in mute approval of the other's bright courage. Then he said:

"The others will be here presently. They'll take you to the hospital. If I can do anything to make you easier till then——"

"Red Injun stuff, hey?" scoffed Bemis from between writhen lips. "Aw, cut it short and do what you're aiming to do!"

"I've done what I aimed to do," said Hardin. "I came here to punish you and to keep you from interfering with my getting Miss Gates safely home. I've done that much. There is nothing more for me to do. Unless," he added, grimly—"unless I find you have been the cause of any worse harm to her than her note told us. If you have, I warn you I'll wait till you are out of hospital and out of prison, and then I'll find you and I'll kill you with my naked hands."

"You're barking up the wrong tree," sneered Tully, forcing his voice to steadiness through the ever-growing inferno of pain. "All I done was to make Cleppy toll her out on to the stoop at Wallace's, and then I took her some-wheres that I c'd keep her safe hid. That was all I done. That was all I aimed to do—unless your Bladen friend gits balky and won't tell where I c'n find what I aim to find."

He broke into a pain-shrill chuckle.

"Lucky for Bladen that he has a he-man to do his fighting for him!" he said, in saturnine amusement. "S'posing he'd of came here hisself to beat me up for stealing his steady comp-ny! He'd 'a' been cut-up dog meat before now, the poor boob! How such a slob c'n make a fine upstanding girl, like teacher, love him enough to hug him and kiss him so bitter, like she done, is more'n I c'n——"

He broke off as a shadow appeared in the sunshine of the open doorway. Very daintily Mars picked his way over the prone and shattered door toward his master. The collie was lame and bleeding. His white paws and his white ruffled shirt-front were asmear with blood. Several super-ficial wounds showed through the tumbled luxuriance of his red-gold coat.

Mars, in his way, had been having well-nigh as strenu-ous a time of it as had his master.

Both men had clean forgotten the existence of the dogs.

The clangor of the triple canine battle in the sloping dooryard had been drowned by the more ferocious din within the cabin.

Now Tully's pain-sick glance roamed from the battered collie out into the yard.

Almost on the threshold lay one of the big black mongrels. In the course of the battle he had made the tactical error of diving too low, in an attempt to crush one of Mars's flying forepaws, and had left his own brain base exposed. Mars had flashed over his diving head and gripped him by the nape of the neck, from above.

Then, heedless of the second dog's rending assaults on himself, the collie had proceeded to break his enemy's neck. After which he had turned his full attention on the dead dog's comrade, in single combat. This second cur lay a little further off, gulping his last spasmodic breaths, his jugular severed.

Yes, Mars had given a good account of himself this day. And now he had come merrily back to his master to be petted and praised for his exploits.

But Bruce had no eyes or ears for his collie chum. Dazedly, aghast, he was staring into space, Tully Bemis's words burning into his brain:

"How such a slob c'n make a fine upstanding girl like teacher love him enough to hug and kiss him——!"

It was a lie, of course. Of that Hardin was sure. A dirty insensate Jackson White lie! But it cut into him like vitriol spattered on raw flesh. In a burst of blind fury he wished he had killed Bemis outright, instead of maiming him.

Then he saw that Tully had turned his gaze from the yard and was watching his conqueror's every expression, evidently reading with ease Hardin's raging thoughts. Bemis grinned faintly, joyous malevolence leaping into his swollen eyes.

"Why, I s'posed you knowed!" he exclaimed. "I s'posed ev'rybody down in the Valley knowed they was keeping comp'ny. Fust I see of it was yest'dy when she was coming home from school. He was waiting for her, at the bottom of one of them ledge paths. She comes a-running down the path and he holds out both of his arms to her and she jumps into 'em. She throwed her arms around his spindly neck and then her and him kissed one the other and she——"

"You lie!" flamed Bruce.

"Kissed so hard they bumped his spect'cles off!" chuckled Bemis, savagely exulting in the torment he saw he was causing. "Bust 'em, most likely. She——"

The rest was lost on Hardin. Back into his memory clicked a chance remark of Bladen's at supper:

"My spectacles got knocked off to-day coming home from the Bear Swamp ridge. Lucky they have horn around them, or I'd have to send to Paterson to-morrow for another pair."

Idly, Bruce had wondered how a safe-anchored pair of spectacles could have been knocked off the geologist's nose in the course of a casual walk. He had been about to ask, when Bladen went on to talk of something else. Afterward the trivial matter had slipped Hardin's mind.

Now he understood. Tully could not possibly have invented corroborative detail of the knocked-off spectacles. That at least was true. And it clinched the truth of the rest of the hideous story.

Bruce's heart was dead within him. He had fared forth

[181]

this morning, like some knight of the Round Table, to do battle with this kidnapper, to risk his life for Sibyl's safety and to avenge her ill-treatment. He had done what he had come hither to do. And now, in the midst of his glory of exultance, his adventure had turned to dust and ashes for him.

Truly, it was Bemis and not he who had won the fight! It was Bruce who suffered far more than the smashed mountaineer could know how to suffer. It was Horace Bladen, then, whom his wonder-sweetheart loved! It was the gentle and shambling convalescent who had won her heart—the heart which Bruce Hardin now knew he himself would have risked life and heaven to win.

Dull-eyed he sat there, his ears deaf to Bemis's chuckled elaborations on the theme. His mind refused to register any further outside impressions.

Whether he sat thus stricken for a minute or for a lifetime, he did not know. Suddenly Mars jumped up from licking his own flesh wounds and looked down the trail. Tully's glance followed the dog's. Voices came up to the cabin, and the multiple clump of shod feet on the stony path.

Bruce forced himself to sanity. Getting up and walking with drunken heaviness, he went forth to meet the newcomers.

Wallace had plied the telephone to fine advantage. Within ten minutes from the time when Bruce had started for the mountains there were five men in the Wallace dooryard, ready to follow him thither. As the quintet were about to set out Mrs. Wallace discovered the anonymous printed note, addressed to Bladen, which Bemis had pinned to the front door on his midnight visit.

Horace opened and read it just as a village constable and a laborer came rattling up in a fast-driven car to join the expedition. The seven made for the mountains at top speed, trotting rather than walking. Bladen and Wallace carried shotguns. Two more of the men had pistols. Word had been sent to others of the valley farmers, but there seemed no need now to wait for them. Leaving directions with the flustered Mrs. Wallace to send these on as soon as they should arrive at the farmhouse, the expedition headed for the Ramapos.

Before the hill-climbing could take away their breath, Wallace asked Horace to read to them Bemis's note. Evasively, Horace put him off, saying he could not make haste and read at the same time, but that the gist of the note was that Sibyl was held for ransom at an unnamed spot in the mountains. He did not read the missive aloud, because of innate delicacy as well as bewilderment. The anonymous note ran:

"Mr. Bladen if you want to see yure sweetart alive you will leav a letter on the flat rock at the left of the bear swampp path at the 2d turn from the fork and tell me in it whare the heshin treasure is hid. If i dont get this word in 48 hrs miss Gates is due to be dead. Dont fool me but tell right whare it is so i can find it and when it is find and taken she will be reternd to you. if you want her back play fare with me and leeve directns in full whare the treasure is burried.

No Name.

Bladen frowned in crass perplexity at the writer's assumption that Sibyl was his "sweetart," but attributed the term's use to some idle mountain gossip which might have been occasioned by his rescue of her from Roan Shively's belting. He was far more puzzled as to how Tully should have gotten the wild idea that he knew anything about the Hessian treasure. That seemed to him the most absurd part of the absurd letter.

Up the steeply twisting trail they made their way at a pace which tried sorely Bladen's returning strength and made the shotgun an increasingly heavy burden to carry. Yet he crowded on all possible speed. He was keenly worried as to Bruce Hardin's possible fate, up there in the hostile community lorded over by the redoubtable Tully. Almost as soon as the party began the long climb the far-off sound of a gunshot was borne to them through the sunrise stillnesses of the mountains. They pressed on faster, the same fear at the heart of all.

"Bruce didn't carry a gun!" grunted Wallace, in perturbation. "Not a single thing to fight with, only his own hands. He——"

A second report broke in on his words.

Grimly, with granite faces, the seven hurried on. They were peaceful and law-abiding folk, these valley farmers, and easy to get along with. Yet before now they had stood up for their rights or to redress wrongs, and the memory of those occasions had not died out. They were men who could turn to war as readily as to peace, were the call strong enough.

Up the last steep pitch of the hillside they scurried; toward the crag whereon stood Bemis's cabin. As they rounded the curve below it they came on a huge black dog lying athwart the path; dead. Assuredly Bruce Hardin's practiced boot toe had done its work too well to leave need for further effort.

The sinister dead body jarred and mystified them. On they hastened. The hut was in full view now. In front of it lay a second dead black dog, while the third was sprawled at the threshold. The door was battered in and the doorway gaped blindly open.

In that doorway stood a half-naked man, bloody and battered, his shirt flapping in tatters around his loins, his long hair matted with sweat, his throat discolored and swollen. Beside him stood a blood-streaked collie. The rescue party were having their first view of the fight's two victors.

On they piled, up to the dooryard, babbling excited questions. Bruce Hardin listened, apathetic and dull-eyed as the storm of queries beat about him. Then, wordlessly, he stepped aside, revealing what lay behind him.

The interior of the cabin was a wreck. Against the farthest wall half lay, half sat a horrible figure, almost nude, bloodstained, battered almost past recognition, the swart face bone yellow with agony.

"Tully Bemis," intoned the constable, advancing and slapping the sufferer smartly on the shoulder, "you're my prisoner. I arrest you on a charge of kidnapping and——"

Tully fainted under the heavy slap upon the shoulder of his broken arm. Even a giant physique can stand only so much, and Tully Bemis this day had endured all he had power to.

Bladen had picked up the twisted gun barrel and the

[185]

shivered walnut stock from the doorstep litter. Mutely he held them out for all to see.

"He fired at me," said Bruce, expressionlessly, in reply to a new volley of questions. "I got the gun away from him and I broke down the door with it. Then we fought. That's all. Give me something to put around my shoulders. I'm cold."

He spoke in the dead voice of a hypnotic subject. He was very tired. He wanted to go somewhere and be alone for the rest of his life. He could not bring himself to meet Bladen's eagerly hero-worshiping gaze, lest Horace read in his face the heartbreak he felt must be visible there.

In reply to his command, every coat was yanked off and outthrust to him, but Horace Bladen was the first to proffer a garment for him to wear.

The dawning day had been cold when Mrs. Wilk awakened Horace with Wallace's telephone message. Bladen had dressed in record time. Then as he left the house he had snatched up a sweater of Bruce's from the hall rack. Long before he reached the Bemis cabin he had taken this off as being too warm and too heavy. Now he forced it upon its rightful owner.

Without a word of thanks Bruce accepted it and drew it on, discarding at the same time the hanging shreds of his shirt.

The constable was working over Bemis, having taken the wholly unnecessary precaution to handcuff the swooning man. Now the officer looked up and said, authoritatively:

"Wallace, you've got a gun. I deputize you to stay here and guard the prisoner while the rest of us go on to the Groot woman's cabin for Miss Gates."

Unwillingly Wallace grumbled assent. Then the constable turned to the others.

"Any of you know how to get there?" he asked.

There was a brief pause. Then Bladen said:

"I blundered on to the shack once, by accident. I might possibly be able to find my way there again, from the valley. But I couldn't guarantee to do it from this angle. I'll try, if you like. But——"

"No, thanks," answered the constable. "Folks have 'tried' to get to places they weren't sure of, in these hills, before now, and they had to be found by a search party. Anyone else know better how to find her cabin? I don't, for one. Who does?"

Bladen spoke up eagerly:

"Bruce Hardin knows every inch of the mountains," said he. "You can take us there, can't you, Bruce?"

Hardin turned on him a face infinitely weary and miserable under its blood smears and bruises. He had hoped to be allowed to go home, unseen, now that the only perilous part of the expedition was at an end. He was of no mind to form part of the audience in the reunion scene between the girl he had lost and the man who had won her.

But it appeared that even this paltry consolation was to be denied him. His dead eyes turned from one to another of the party.

"Nobody else know how to get there?" he asked. "All right. Come along."

CHAPTER

14

AN exclamation of amusement from the doorway made him turn. Ethan Wallace was standing there on watch, gun in hand.

"Say!" Wallace informed all and sundry, "I just saw something shin down from that pine tree over yonder and slink off in the woods. I only got a fair glimpse at it for a second. But that was enough. It was Roan Shively. I figger he's heard a rumpus here and he clumb the tree to see it without gitting mixed up in it. Yep, that's been it, as sure as shooting. He's seen what he wanted to, and he's off to spread the news how Tully's licked and busted to pieces and arrested. You boys won't have much trouble from Jackson Whites interfering with you on the way home. He——"

"He'll get the news to Auntie Groot's cabin!" cried

Bruce, coming galvanically to life. "And then the Lord only knows where they'll hide Miss Gates or what they'll do to her. Come on!"

Fatigue and heartbreak forgotten in this pressing need for action, he led the way across the clearing and into the ridge-top forest, walking fast, running whenever the ground was smooth enough for such a risk.

The others crashed along through the undergrowth, keeping up as best they could. But after the first half-mile the fleetest of them was far behind and was following with difficulty the ever more distant sweatered figure that plunged so heedlessly ahead.

Thus it was that Bruce came out at last on the edge of the low eminence above the cuplike hollow in whose center the Groot cabin stood. At each of the shack's four sides lounged a slender and ragged figure. The four Blue-eyed Niggers were still faithfully on guard.

At sight of the oncoming Hardin they grouped together threateningly, and one of them called a jumbled sentence of warning through the window to those inside. From within the cabin arose a snarling sound as of an angry cat.

Down the slope slid Hardin, to the dooryard of the shack. With no hesitation he made for the four men who guarded the single doorway. At sight of his blood-streaked face and blazing eyes they shrank back close to the door. As he kept on toward them this door was flung open. On the threshold appeared Auntie Groot, holding threateningly above her head a black kettle from whose spout issued a cloud of steam.

The old woman had snatched up from the stove her favorite weapon. The cat glare in her ancient eyes proved she was ready and eager to make deadly use of it. Her face showed signs of her last night's potations. But the withered mummy hand did not shake as it wielded the heavy kettle.

At sight of her the four guards made way, opening a path for her to advance upon her unwelcome visitor. Heedless of her menace, Bruce forged ahead. Now he was within two steps of the door-stone. Auntie Groot swung back the kettle to hurl it and its scalding contents full in his face.

Then, directly behind the old woman, into the open doorway stepped Sibyl Gates. At a glance she understood the peril. With a single downward sweep of her sinuous young arm she struck the brandished kettle from its wielder's aged clasp.

Auntie Groot, expecting no such move from her hitherto docile captive, was taken utterly by surprise. The kettle was poised for the throw when Sibyl's hand struck it down. To the door-stone it fell with a clatter, the boiling water sloshing in every direction—over the bare feet and the shins of the four bellowing Blue-eyed Niggers and over the bare and wizened toes of the old woman—almost everywhere, in fact, except on the man for whom it had been intended.

With a screech of animal fury and hurt, Auntie Groot whizzed about and clawed with her long nails at Sibyl's face. Bruce, his hand gripping her emaciated shoulder, drew her back from the feline assault on the girl, barely in time to keep the talon-like fingers from finding their mark in the soft flesh.

The four Blue-eyed Niggers drew stealthily in on him. From the pocket of one of them a crooked-bladed knife slithered into view. Then another of them called out a guttural word and pointed upward. The constable and his party had reached the ridge top and were beginning to cascade down into the hollow.

At sight of the armed valley men, and not knowing how many might be behind them, the four guards scuttled off in every direction. The undergrowth swallowed them up as it might have swallowed a covey of skulking quail.

Balked of her laudable effort to disfigure the face of the girl who had knocked the kettle from her hand, Auntie Groot spun about to attack the man who had caught hold of her shoulder. Then, as she wheeled, her ancient toothless jaw fell slack and she staggered backward as though she had been struck.

Down upon her from the ridge were sweeping a swarm of men, the badged and pistoled constable in the forefront, Bladen close behind him, shotgun in hand, and, seemingly, an endless succession of other intruders in their wake.

Auntie Groot's century-old life dread had at last been fulfilled. The Law had found her out. The folk of the valley were storming her hut, even as, seventy years earlier, she had seen them raid the mountains in quest of a half-breed murderer.

Gone was the woman's life-long seclusion. The secret of her abode and of her own life was no longer a secret. Again and again she had dreamed of this hour, on nights of fever, and had wakened shuddering and cursing. Now it had come!

Palsied, her amazing spryness and strength mysteriously drained in a single instant, she pressed back into the house, past Sibyl, and strove to shut and bar the door behind her.

[191]

The constable caught the closing door with his outstretched palm and shoved it wide, well-nigh upsetting the frail old creature behind it.

Into the room he stalked magisterially, the others at his back. Sibyl, in a gush of pity for her forlorn old jailer's plight, followed. Bruce stood in the shadows.

Auntie Groot had retreated from the door. Now she barricaded herself behind the rickety table, reinforcing her position by kneeling on the cracked old box which served as a chair for it. She bore a humiliating likeness to a treed alley cat.

The constable advanced upon her, coming around the table toward where she knelt. Seldom did he get such chances to exert his super-legal authority as were piling thick and fast upon him this morning.

"Betje Groot," he intoned, reaching out his hand and placing it majestically on her shrinking pipe stem of an arm, "you are my prisoner. I arrest you for aiding and abetting the crime of kidnapping, and for—— *Ouch!* You damn hell cat!"

This last was no portion of his or any other officer's formula of arrest, yet it was declaimed with infinitely more fervor and lung power than all the rest of his harangue put together.

Auntie Groot had resented his familiar touch on her arm by bringing down five hooked fingers with skilled force upon his detaining hand. There was a sweeping and clawing motion to her gesture. Its net result was a parallel of deep red stripes on the officer's plump handback.

With a brief return to her former eerie spryness, Auntie

Groot leaped back from him toward the stove. The constable, abrim with righteous indignation, made after her. At his first step his shin came into cruelly hard contact with the corner of the cracked box that stood half beside and half under the edge of the deal table.

His frayed temper stirred to a blaze by this second painful mishap within the space of two seconds, the constable was guilty of what our whimsical Jersey Dutch ancestors were wont to term "wooden swearing."

In other words, he drew back his heavy boot and bestowed upon the offending box a hearty and heartfelt kick.

The constable instantly let forth another roar. The greasy and supposedly empty old packing-box was heavy enough to send a throb of hurt up his whole leg.

The box, too, had suffered from that mighty kick. The jar of the collision with the constable's boot sent it slithering out into the room, beyond the shelter of the table.

It did more. It split and shivered the rotting old boards and snapped several of the rusty nails. A whole side of the box fell away, in splintered sections.

Within was revealed the side of a slightly smaller box, of stained and dented oak, iron-bound and studded with greenish brass nails.

As the others looked in wonder at the odd sight, Bladen came forward and knelt in front of the box. He pointed eagerly at a mark burnt into the exposed oaken side.

"Why, look!" he exclaimed. "That's the 'broad arrow' branded into the wood. It's the British government's official mark. It has been the British mark, for centuries. I wonder how a——"

With a wildcat squall, Auntie Groot flung herself at him, menacing his bent head with a flatiron she had snatched from the stove.

"*Vaul dief*," she yowled, foaming at the lips. "*Hont!* It is *mine!* Keep your hands off it!"

As she shrieked the rabid command she hurled down the hot flatiron, with all her insane power, at his unguarded head.

The flung flatiron might well have found its mark, despite the ancient fallacy that no woman can throw straight; in which case Horace Bladen would have been carried back from the mountains with a fractured skull.

But almost before it left the frantic old woman's hand Hardin, who had come forward and stood at her elbow, struck it aside with a wide sweep of his palm-open hand. The missile clumped to the floor, barely missing the constable's roomy feet.

There was an instant of turmoil. The constable ended the episode by lifting the screeching and kicking and scratching crone bodily in his arms and bearing her to the windowless cubbyhole behind the cabin's main room. Into this abode of odds and ends he thrust her for safekeeping, and he closed and bolted its door after her.

"Let her stay there till she quiets down," he said, nursing a new set of scratches on his hand and wrist. "No use taking her down to jail while that crazy fit is on her. She'll wear herself out in a minute or two. She's too old and weak to keep it up. When she's tired she'll be as easy to take along as a sick kitten. Now, then, what's all this talk about broad arrows, Mr. Bladen? That's what seemed to rile her worst. What's the point of it?"

[194]

"No," spoke up Sibyl Gates, her brow clearing after a moment of quick thought. "No. That wasn't what excited her. It was because Mr. Bladen was prying at that chest. That was what made her so furious. The broad arrow had nothing to do with it."

"But——"

"And," went on the girl, excitedly, "don't you see? This was something she had been guarding—something she had been hiding from everyone. She chose the very cleverest way to do it, too. In almost all the Jackson White shacks I've been in there is at least one more or less decayed packing-box that does duty as a seat. Most of them are empty. Some of them are full of junk that there's no room for elsewhere. Anyhow, the sight of a battered old packing-box wouldn't rouse any more interest or curiosity up here than a rocking-chair would in a valley house. So when Auntie Groot had something to hide she hid it in that—on Poe's principle that the simplest hiding-place is the hardest to find. From the looks of it, it must have been here for ever so many years. Perhaps for half a century or more. It——"

"*I* know!" cried Horace Bladen, in sudden noisy enlightenment. "I get your drift now! You mean it is the Hessian treasure! Old Groot left it for her to keep. She's been watching over it ever since. People have hunted from one end of these mountains to the other for it. They've hunted everywhere except in a rotting packing-box-chair that is like a hundred other rotting packing-box-chairs in the Ramapo shacks. She's a genius! No wonder she came at me like a wildcat when I started to examine it!"

As he spoke he attacked the decayed old crate as if it were a mortal enemy. Under his tugging hands its ancient boards tore loose with comparative ease. At last its fragments lay on the dirty floor. There, revealed to all eyes, stood the dented oaken chest with its iron bindings and its verdigris-green brass nails. Atop it was a squat little casket, scarce four inches high by perhaps twelve inches long and broad—a casket of mildewed morocco leather, stained black by time and dampness and fastened with a tarnished silver padlock.

"The British-army pay-chest that was on its way to Morristown with the money for the troops there!" exulted Bladen, harking back to the yellowed letter Bruce Hardin had read aloud the week before. "And Major Hough's casket with the cash and the jewelry he told his wife to send him. They're HERE!"

At once a turmoil of voices arose in query and comment and exclamation. So loud were they that they drowned out the diminishing volume of outcry from Auntie Groot in the cubbyhole back room.

Not a man there but had heard the rumor of Hessian treasure buried somewhere in the Ramapos, though nobody there had given real credence to the improbable yarn. All pressed around the chest and the casket, avidly, alive with curiosity and with the gold lust that lies dormant in every human mind's recesses.

Bruce Hardin alone took no part in the uproar. The fact that the treasure was actually found made no faintest difference to him in his present mood. The collapse of the world, and of the universe as well, would have made little more difference to him. All he asked of God or man was a chance to get away by himself, to confront this crushing of all his life's hopes, out of sight of the girl he loved and had lost, out of sight of the triumphant man who had won her.

The way to the door was clear. Nobody was noticing him. Nobody had eyes or ears or thoughts for anything but the treasure. There was no need for him to stay longer. Sibyl was free. She was in no danger, with this posse of neighbors to escort her home. At last he had the right to be alone with his sorrow.

Unobtrusively he made his way to the door. On the threshold he paused. Out of the din he heard the constable's pompous voice declaring:

"Whatever these boxes may contain, the contents belong to the state. That's the law, you know. So——"

"It is nothing of the kind," denied Bruce, hotly, turning back into the room and confronting the policeman with all the authority he could muster.

He knew well that the constable's knowledge of the finer points of the law, outside his own province, was wholly negligible. He knew him, too, for the sort of man who is easily impressed by another's firm show of knowledge and of authority.

Bruce himself had not the remotest acquaintance with the law governing treasure trove, nor even if such law existed. But he did know that Horace Bladen was poor, that the convalescent had barely enough income to support himself in modest comfort, that he could not hope to support a wife decently on his present means.

The possession of this treasure might make Bladen a rich man. It might, incidentally, provide a hundred luxuries and necessities for Sibyl and relieve her of the grinding poverty and the pitiful economies and makeshifts which scourge the path of a poor man's wife. It was for Sibyl, therefore, that he plunged into the discussion, even as it was for Sibyl he had plunged into the murderous fight with Tully Bemis that morning.

"It is nothing of the kind," he repeated, confronting the officer and speaking as if from vast legal lore. "That treasure-trove clause applies only to natural mineral wealth discovered on government land. As a public official you surely must know that. Well, *this* treasure is not 'natural mineral wealth' and this is not government land. Thus, the treasure goes to its finder. Mr. Bladen is the finder. It was he who discovered and classified these two boxes inside the packing-case. By all right, and by law, the valuables are his and his alone, unless he cares to reward the rest of you in some slight way for being the indirect causes of his finding it, which I am sure he will. This discovery comes directly under the head of 'Personal Rights and Privileges, as Opposed to Riparian Rights and Torts,' " improvised Hardin from fragmentary terms picked up during an unsuccessful six months, years ago, at law school.

"As a constable, you are no doubt familiar with that platitudinous valetudinarian clause in the statutes of the state of New Jersey."

Immensely impressed, the constable tried to look as though he had just recalled to memory the familiar clause in question, and mumbled sheepish affirmation. Bladen and Sibyl stared dumfounded at Bruce, they being the only members of the party to understand the rank absurdity of his solemn exhortation.

It was Sibyl's first clear look at Hardin, in the interval of rush and excitement, since she had knocked aside the kettle aimed at him. At that time the rising sun had been at his back. Now she saw not only the utter weary hopelessness of his face, but its bruises and the drying blood flecked here and there upon it. Her heart went out to him in a great wave of almost motherly love in his misery and physical discomfort.

But before she could speak Hardin had knelt beside the money chest and was fumbling with its rusted clasps. Bladen turned his own attention to the smaller and very much lighter casket.

"Here, one of you," Hardin bade the close-packed group that crowded around the boxes, "go out into the yard and get that hatchet I saw stuck in the chopping-block. Bring it here."

In ten seconds an officious neighbor was handing him a chipped and decrepit hatchet. Weak-seeming as the thing was, yet it was sufficiently sound to smash each of the rust-eaten padlocks of the chest with a single sharp blow. Laying it down, Bruce sought to raise the iron-bound lid. The dust and damp of nearly a century and a half had welded it shut. He picked up the hatchet again, wielding it skillfully against the protruding lower edge of the lid.

Creaking, groaning a weird protest against the violation of its long sanctity, the top of the chest parted company with its rust-caked hinges. The interior was exposed to the view of the circle of hysterically eager eyes. From the cubbyhole came the ever-furious voice of Auntie Groot, now sunk almost to a hoarse whisper.

Perhaps in each onlooker's brain was a vision of high-piled golden guineas interspersed with ingots and with strings of pearls and blazing diamonds. At first glimpse of the interior of the chest there was a multiple gasp of dis-

[199]

appointment. Hardin alone did not join in the wordless chorus of chagrin, partly because he could not have summoned a spark of interest, just then, in all the wealth of the universe; partly because he had shifted the position of the chest before striking off its decaying locks, and he knew by the ease of its movement that the box could not well contain much internal weight.

CHAPTER

15

A MASS of papers, yellow and stained, rewarded the gaze of the onlookers. There were packets on packets of these papers, some large, some small, each parcel bound in rotting and discolored official tape. The seals were blackened blotches. Packet after packet of legal-looking papers, with here and there a parcel of letters, and at the bottom great sheaves of printed slips, with figures inked faintly upon them.

This was the contents of the Hessian treasure-chest, theme of a century's speculation and search, goal of Tully Bemis's life ambition. Here was the hoard wherewith Bruce had hoped to enrich his friend who had won Sibyl! One more of Bruce's hopes turned to ashes.

He and Bladen and Sibyl, by common consent, began to

pick up one packet after another, breaking the rotted tape and straining their eyes to decipher the mildewed and faded writings thereon. The constable grabbed for a sheaf of printed slips and pored over the topmost handful of them.

Little by little the rummagers learned the true contents of the chest which Groot and Mann and Devries had stolen so craftily and which had been hidden from gaze since before the end of the American Revolution.

There were letters and expresses—some personal, some official—to officers in the Morristown expedition and to Morristown Tories. There were military orders addressed to the British commanding officer and to certain British spies, etc., quartered in or near Morristown in 1780 and 1781—folk whose bodies had long since crumbled to dust.

But the chief contents of the chest was that huge sheaf of printed blanks with figures inked into them. These were orders on the local military paymaster and on the British paymaster-general in New York for carrying sums of cash, representing each soldier's and officer's pay.

Such bits of scrip had passed current as cash in British army circles at the time, and had been accepted as such by shops and by individuals. The British authorities in New York had been too wise to ship a vast sum of actual money across a stretch of hostile country when pay checks would serve the purpose equally well.

"Mad Anthony Wayne's" riders had swooped down upon the Hessian escort under the impression that the chest was full of gold and silver for the paying of the Morristown soldiers. Had they secured the chest, they would have found themselves in possession of several thousand slips of paper—paper which could be cashed or exchanged only inside the British lines.

"Don't you see?" Bladen finished a terse explanation to that effect. "To the British troops this represented thousands of guineas in money. To anyone else it was of no more value than an unendorsed check drawn on Ethan Wallace would be to me. These enormous wads of pay slips have the same present cash value to us, or to anyone else, as a treasury order signed in 3000 B. C. by Pharaoh would have. It's waste paper. Moldy waste paper, at that. These letters and other documents were packed into the half-empty chest as the shortest and surest way of getting them from the British in New York to the British in Morristown."

He spoke with forced lightness, though, like all the rest, he had a sense of almost nauseating disappointment and reaction. His chapfallen expression was reflected on his hearers' faces.

"When these pay checks were drawn," he pursued, "they called for enough money to make all of us fairly rich. To-day, all of them put together wouldn't buy a postage stamp. They can't even be sold as curios. The curio market is flooded with such checks. As for the letters—especially the private ones—they may be of some interest, later, to read. But that is all. I'm sorry."

He fell silent. Sibyl Gates broke the glum stillness by picking up the small casket and handing it to Bruce.

"Why not open this, too?" she asked him. "It is too light to hold much. But it may be amusing to——"

"Let Bladen open it for you," suggested Bruce, none too graciously. "It belongs to him as the finder."

He turned toward Horace. The geologist had just opened at random one of the frayed yellow letters from the heap he and Bruce had tossed out on to the floor. He was reading aloud its first faded sentences. It was from an irate Tory father to his son at Morristown, who, it seemed, had been spending too much money. The letter began in a peppery style of denunciation. It seemed to tickle the overstrained senses of Bladen's hearers, and he read on.

Not wanting to interrupt him, Bruce carried the casket and the hatchet over to the stronger light of the doorway. Sibyl followed and stood over him while he struck off the fragile old lock and pried up the lid. The others had not observed, in their hysterical amusement at the angry old Tory's letter which Bladen was spelling out.

Atop the open contents of the casket was a letter, sealed and wrapped in several strands of glossy black hair.

"It must be from Major Hough's wife, inventorying the things she had put in here," suggested Bruce. "Shall I open it first, or——?"

"No!" begged the girl, laying a restraining hand on his as he made as if to break the seal. "She—she must have loved him—if she pulled out strands of her own long hair to bind the letter, after she had sealed it. We have no right to read it, have we?—the letter a wife sent, with all the money she could raise, to her absent husband?"

Obediently, Hardin laid aside the age-stained letter with its wrappings of deathless black hair. From the casket he lifted a handful of taped papers. They were British military pay checks—probably a salary advance secured by his wife from New York headquarters—made out to "Major Malcolm Hough, in quarters at Morristown."

Below were three checks, drawn by "Barbara Hough" for varying sums and on three banks.

"Poor woman!" commented Sibyl. "You see, she went around to every bank where she or her husband had an account, and drew it all out. She took literally his demand for all the money she could raise. And then, look at this!"

She took from the casket seven other bank checks, all made out to Hough, and with different signatures.

"She went around among his friends, you see," she explained, with swift feminine intuition, "and she borrowed from all of them, to make up the sum he told her to raise."

"Yes," agreed Bruce, unimpressed, "but I wish for your sake she had collected the money in cash for him, instead of checks."

"For *my* sake?" repeated Sibyl, puzzled. "Why, it isn't mine! *I* didn't discover it. It was Mr. Bladen. He——"

"Quite so," Hardin cut her short, nettled by her seeming secretiveness and loath to pursue the painful theme.

He drew forth the last article in the casket—a tiny silken package, round and compact, evidently made from part of a handkerchief-muffler, now frazzled and worn and stained. It was held together by a bit of gold wire fastened neatly and firmly about it and fastened at both points of juncture by a thick seal.

As Bruce turned the little silk bundle over in his torn hand the thin gold wire parted, just beneath one of the seals. The ancient seal itself sloughed off of its insecure silken anchorage. One end of the folded silk fell open.

Hardin turned the parcel around to explore the aperture. At his first motion something leaped out of the folds and whizzed in a flaming parabola through the sunlit air, coming to rest with a metallic click in the kicked-up earth of the dooryard.

As it flew, the rays of the new-risen sun had smitten it. The thing had blazed into a meteor of scintillating crimson light, dazzling to behold.

Even now, as it lay in the muck of the dooryard, it gave back the sunlight in a flare of riotous crimson glory.

Sibyl cried out in astonished delight at the wondrous beauty of it. Bruce, more practical and less interested, stooped and picked it out of the dirt.

It was a ruby ring, set in carven antique gold. The stone was perhaps six carats in weight. It had been cut by a master craftsman, to bring forth all its fire and loveliness.

Apparently Major Hough's devoted wife had added this last family gem to the list of valuables sent by her to relieve her husband's sudden need for funds. Such a jewel, even in Revolutionary times, would have found ready purchase or could have been pledged for a large sum to any professional money-lender.

Perhaps thinking her husband could drive a sharper bargain with such army usurers than could she at a New York pawnshop, she had sent it on to him instead of selling or pawning it and forwarding to him a draft for its purchase price or for its pledging. It may have been that she hoped he might not have need to sell it in order to raise the money he needed and that she gave him thus a chance to keep it, while she herself obeyed his order to send him all the wealth she could scrape together.

In any case, more than one hundred and forty years later, here was the magnificent ruby in its heavy antique setting, snuggling in Bruce Hardin's callous palm. He blinked at it dazedly. Then at Sibyl's exclamation of joy he handed it to her.

Over and over in her white hands she turned it, reveling, woman-like, in the flame and glow and pulsing beauty of it. To try its effect the better, she slipped it momentarily on to one of her slender fingers, whence the ring hung loose and heavy.

On the setting, close to the stone, sparkled in the sun a drop of blood. In the effort to pry open the casket lid, Hardin's cut palm had begun to bleed again. With a little cry of sympathy and self-reproach Sibyl wheeled on him.

"Oh," she exclaimed, "you're hurt! And you never told me! I was so selfish. I——"

Shamefacedly he hid his hands behind him, like a sulky schoolboy.

"I must have barked the flesh on that lid when I opened the box," he said. "Please don't bother about it. I'm only sorry I smeared your ring with it. I——"

"It isn't my ring," she denied. "It isn't mine at all. You found it. Never mind that, now! I want you to tell me about yourself. That's a million times more important. What has happened to you? I didn't want to ask, where the others were. I knew you wouldn't like to talk about it. But you've had something terrible happen to you! I know it. Your face is hurt and there is blood on it and a bruise. And your hands——"

"I got into a squabble with your friend Tully Bemis," he said, lightly, "and he left his trade mark on me. It's nothing worth speaking of. Please don't——"

[207]

"But I must!" she urged, her eyes full of tears, her hand on his arm. "I know what has happened. I know what *must* have happened. You fought him for my sake and it was you who brought these people here to release me. I know it was. Oh, there aren't any words to thank you with!"

"Let's let it go at that," he begged, in red embarrassment. "I didn't do anything worth your remembering. Bladen and I are chums, you know. And now I'm going home, if you don't mind. I'm glad if——"

"Auntie Groot woke up only a few minutes before you got here," pursued the girl. "And as she was putting on the kettle and stirring up the fire she told me how you went up to the Shivelys' the other day, and how you thrashed Roan for what he tried to do to me, and how you frightened all the Jackson Whites into leaving me alone. She said that was why the four Blue-eyed Niggers had to stay on guard. No Jackson White would raise a hand to help Bemis, after what you had done. She was hateful about it. But it made me so glad—and so ashamed! I never can thank you enough. Never! And then on top of it all, the things you've done for me this morning——"

"Please!" he begged once more, in sick deprecation of her eager praise. "*Please* don't! I've just reminded you that Bladen and I are chums. He'd have done as much for me, if he could, as I've just done for him and for his happiness. He——"

"I don't understand!" she faltered, her upraised face as pitiful as a misunderstood child's. "I——"

"I think you do," he corrected gently, yet with that same earlier feeling of contempt for her disingenuousness in seeking to keep her love for Horace a secret from Horace's best friend.

She had taken off the great shimmering ruby as she talked and she was holding it out to him, her dainty face flushed and tearful. Bruce waved back the proffered ring.

"It's Bladen's," he said, "not mine. If you don't want him to sell it, tell him I say to give it to you for an engagement ring. And—and all the luck and happiness in God's world to both of you!"

He turned about abruptly and strode toward the ridge. The girl stared speechlessly after him. She took an impulsive step forward and, finding her voice at last, called, brokenly:

"Bruce! Come back! I——"

The ridge-top bushes had swallowed him. As she made as though to follow, in a hopeless attempt to catch up with his rapid strides, something darted out of the shack and bounded past her. It was the collie. Turning from his interested sniffing among the ruck of scattered old papers, he had heard his master's receding stride and was off in a rush to follow him.

"Mars!" called Sibyl, coaxingly, as the red-gold dog sprang past her toward the ridge.

Mars did not so much as check his gallop. He was fond of Sibyl. At Bruce's orders he had even consented to spend part of his days at the mountain school with her. But to-day Hardin had given him no such command. Thus the collie felt himself at liberty to deafen his ears to her half-sobbing summons and to follow his god.

On through the forest Bruce Hardin strode, heartsick

and weary of life. In another half-minute there was a pattering behind him and a cold nose was thrust lovingly into his hand, Mars was grinning delightedly up into his haggard face, the plumed tail waving, his hurts forgotten in the fact that he and his master were alone together on another mountain walk.

Hardin stooped and caught the classic head roughly between his lacerated palms.

"Old friend!" he muttered. "There'll be only the two of us left. A man's chum—a man's sweetheart—everything a man clings to—they all drift away from him, don't they? What's left? His dog! His dog is the only thing that will stick to him always! The dog whose love is 'greater than the love of women.' I thank God for you, old comrade of mine!"

Ashamed of his maudlin outburst, Bruce hurried along toward the nearest trail by which he could descend to the valley and to his own home.

Arrived there, he evaded Mrs. Wilk's torrent of queries, merely telling her Sibyl was safe and would be at the Wallace house in a little while. Of his own disheveled condition he refused to talk. But he bade her look to Mars's cuts and to wash and bandage them.

Going upstairs, he bathed and then ministered as best he could to his various hurts. Then, dressing afresh, he went forth to his neglected farm-work.

He did not come home at noon, but remained toiling in his more distant fields until sunset, seeking by heavy physical labor to still the pain at his heart.

Early dusk was falling when he turned his steps homeward. Then and then only did he realize he was sick with exhaustion. He had eaten nothing for more than twenty-four hours. He had strained muscles and nerves and heart in a life-and-death battle. On top of this he had worked in the fields for twelve hot hours; ever goaded to dull torture by the knowledge of his loss of Sibyl.

Exhausted, enervated, his steps heavy and dragging, he made his way home. There, to his relief, he found Bladen was out and had been out most of the day. He could guess where the fortunate lover was likely to be at this twilight hour. Seating himself at the supper table, Bruce forced himself to eat the meal Mrs. Wilk set before him. But most of it went to Mars, who lay, as ever, on the floor to the left of his master's chair.

Supper over, he went out on the porch and sat down in the warm springtime dusk for his evening smoke. As he sat there, Mars at his feet, a car stopped at the head of the lane leading to the house. A man got out and the car went on down the highroad. Even at that distance Bruce recognized Horace Bladen's lanky form and awkward gait. So Bladen had not been with Sibyl, after all, Bruce reflected, sneering at the geologist for not spending every leisure minute in her company as he himself yearned to do.

"Hello!" Bladen greeted him, coming up the steps and sitting down beside his chum. "Where have you been all day? I looked all over for you before I went to Paterson. Conklin gave me a lift home. What a day!"

"Yes," agreed Hardin, dryly, "it *has* been a wakeful day."

"I don't mean up in the mountains," said Horace. "I

meant down at Paterson at the hospital and at the jail and in the courtroom. Want to hear about it? It's pretty interesting."

"Fire away," vouchsafed Bruce, wearily, and in total dearth of interest.

Bladen caught the note of utter weariness, and accordingly cut down his story to the bare outline, reserving the details for a time when his hearer should show more concern in the matter.

"Well," he began, "Bemis was carted down to the prison ward of the Paterson Hospital. So was Auntie Groot. By the time we let her out of that back room she was in a state of senile collapse. Came near dying of sheer fatigue before we could get her to the hospital. It wasn't till late this afternoon that the police could brace her up enough from her stupor to get her to talk. Even then she wouldn't say a word till the chief promised her she'd get off lightly by coming across clean, and that she'd get back all the sooner to her beloved home-shack. At that she loosened up and talked.

"Here's the idea in a nutshell. Old Man Groot—the original Hessian Groot, you know—was her grandfather. After everyone else of his kin was dead and he was bedridden, she took all the care of him. He didn't die till she was about twenty. Just a little while before he died he told her where he and the two other Hessians had buried the chest and the casket. He made her swear never to tell and he made her go at night and lug them to the cabin. It was he who gave her the idea of getting hold of a strong packing-case to hide them in and to avoid suspicion by keeping it in plain sight in the cabin and using it as a chair.

"She kept her oath and she kept the secret. I gather that

[212]

years and years of living with the treasure made her grow
to love it, as some sort of fetish or idol. Anyhow, she never
told; and she never even opened the chest or the casket.
That's the funniest part of all. The chief asked her why
she didn't open them. She said she was 'afraid Granther
Groot's ghost would strangle her, like he swore he would
if she opened 'em.' Apparently they had gotten to be a sort
of fetish with old Groot himself, you see, in the sixty or
seventy years he had watched over them before he died.

"The chief asked her about Tully Bemis. It seems she's
really fond of Tully, for some reason. Yet she could never
bring herself to tell him the secret—either because she
thought he'd kill her and steal the treasure, or else for
fear 'Granther Groot's ghost' would punish her for breaking her oath. She says the oath is no use now that there
is really no treasure at all. So she can speak. Poor old dame!
One of the doctors down there told me he doesn't believe
she'll live to go back to her cabin or anywhere else. He
says she's kept herself alive to guard the treasure. The reaction will be too much for her, he thinks. Lord! but Tully
Bemis was raving when he found out the treasure was such
a hoax! Crippled as he was, it took three men to hold him
down in his cot when the chief told him about it. The same
doctor told me Tully is more likely to go to an asylum than
to prison. He——"

Out of the dusk appeared a slender white-clad figure,
walking toward the porch. At sight of her Mars's plumed
tail began to smite the veranda boards and Bruce's heart
began to smite his ribs with far harder and more painful
iteration.

"It's Sibyl Gates," said Bladen. "I'm going in to see if

[213]

any supper is left. I'll be out presently. I'm half starved."

He went indoors as he spoke. Bruce would have followed him, but already the girl had come so close to the steps that she could not have failed to note his rudeness in not stopping to welcome her.

"Horace will be out in a few minutes," he said, going perfunctorily forward to meet her. "Won't you sit down till he——"

"I didn't come to see Mr. Bladen," she said, very quietly but with much determination. "I came to see you."

"But why? I——"

"Because I knew you wouldn't come to see me. There was no use in sending for you. I told Mrs. Wallace I was going for a little walk. I never called on a man before," she went on, embarrassedly. "But this time I had to come. In books and sometimes in real life a silly misunderstanding so often breaks people's lives to pieces. That was why I had to forget conventionality and come here to see you this evening."

She paused. Hardin looked perplexedly at her through the soft dusk.

"Well?" he asked, wearily, dreading some speech of banal gratitude or a further argument about the possession of the ruby. "Well? What is it?"

He realized the question was ungracious. But to save his soul he could not say more.

"Mr. Wallace told me some things Tully Bemis said," she resumed—"things he said while Mr. Wallace was there, guarding him, this morning. Tully said he had told you the same things. Bruce, how could you have believed such hideous stories? For you *did* believe them, Bruce. That was why you spoke to me as you did, about Mr. Bladen and about the ruby. It hurt me so, to have you speak so! To have you look at me as you did! *Why* did you?"

The man was staring dumfoundedly at her. His brain was awhirl. The sudden lift from blank misery left him speechless. All he could do was to catch both her hands in a grip that hurt and continue to stare at her.

"Bruce," she asked, her sweet voice so low that he guessed rather than heard the whispered words, "do you still want me to wear the ruby, as—as an engagement ring? Because if you do you'll have to have it cut down to fit me. I——"

"Well!" announced Bladen, from the doorway, "didn't I get through supper in record time? It was cold and clammy, anyhow. So I——"

"Go back and eat some more of it!" shouted Bruce, finding his voice at last in a pæan of ecstasy. "Then stay there and eat the plates and Mrs. Wilk. You—you don't come on in this scene at all, you old four-eyed blunderer! I'm getting engaged!"